11

Strike the Blood

The Fugitive Fourth Primogenitor

Gakuto Mikumo

Illustration by **Manyako**

Kojou Akatsuki
The Fourth Primogenitor
The world's mightiest—and
laziest—vampire

Yukina Himeragi
Sword Shaman
The Lion King Agency's
beautiful observer

Asagi Aiba
Cyber Empress
Gorgeous, selfish
high school cyber genius

Motoki Yaze
Hyper Adapter
Cheerful classmate
or two-faced jester?

Natsuki Minamiya
Witch of the Void
Vainglorious, noble teacher

Kiriha Kisaki
Priestess of the Six Blades
Beautiful, menacing, jet-black
wielder of the demon spear

Contents

Design / Hirokazu Watanabe (2725, Inc.)

STRIKE THE BLOOD

THE FUGITIVE FOURTH PRIMOGENITOR

11

GAKUTO MIKUMO

ILLUSTRATION BY
MANYAKO

YEN ON

NEW YORK

STRIKE THE BLOOD, Volume 11
GAKUTO MIKUMO

Translation by Jeremiah Bourque
Cover art by Manyako

This book is a work of fiction. Names, characters, places, and incidents are
the product of the author's imagination or are used fictitiously. Any resemblance to
actual events, locales, or persons, living or dead, is coincidental.

SUTORAIKU ZA BURADDO Vol.11
©GAKUTO MIKUMO 2014
First published in Japan in 2014 by KADOKAWA CORPORATION, Tokyo.
English translation rights arranged with KADOKAWA CORPORATION, Tokyo,
through Tuttle-Mori Agency, Inc., Tokyo.

English translation © 2019 by Yen Press, LLC

Yen On
1290 Avenue of the Americas
New York, NY 10104

Visit us at yenpress.com
facebook.com/yenpress
twitter.com/yenpress
yenpress.tumblr.com
instagram.com/yenpress

First Yen On Edition: January 2019

Yen On is an imprint of Yen Press, LLC.
The Yen On name and logo are trademarks of Yen Press, LLC.

The publisher is not responsible for websites (or their content) that are not owned by the publisher.

Library of Congress Cataloging-in-Publication Data
Names: Mikumo, Gakuto, author. | Manyako, illustrator. | Bourque, Jeremiah, translator.
Title: Strike the blood / Gakuto Mikumo, Manyako ; translation by Jeremiah Bourque.
Other titles: Sutoraiku za buraddo. English
Description: New York, NY : Yen On, 2016–
Identifiers: LCCN 2015041522 | ISBN 9780316345477 (v. 1 : pbk.) |
ISBN 9780316345491 (v. 2 : pbk.) | ISBN 9780316345514 (v. 3 : pbk.) |
ISBN 9780316345538 (v. 4 : pbk.) | ISBN 9780316345569 (v. 5 : pbk.) |
ISBN 9780316345583 (v. 6 : pbk.) | ISBN 9780316562652 (v. 7 : pbk.) |
ISBN 9780316442084 (v. 8 : pbk.) | ISBN 9780316442107 (v. 9 : pbk.) |
ISBN 9780316442121 (v. 10 : pbk.) | ISBN 9780316442145 (v. 11 : pbk.)
Subjects: CYAC: Vampires—Fiction. | BISAC: FICTION / Science Fiction / Adventure.
Classification: LCC PZ7.1.M555 Su 2016 | DDC [Fic]—dc23
LC record available at http://lccn.loc.gov/2015041522

ISBNs: 978-0-316-44214-5 (paperback)
978-0-316-44215-2 (ebook)

1 3 5 7 9 10 8 6 4 2

LSC-C

Printed in the United States of America

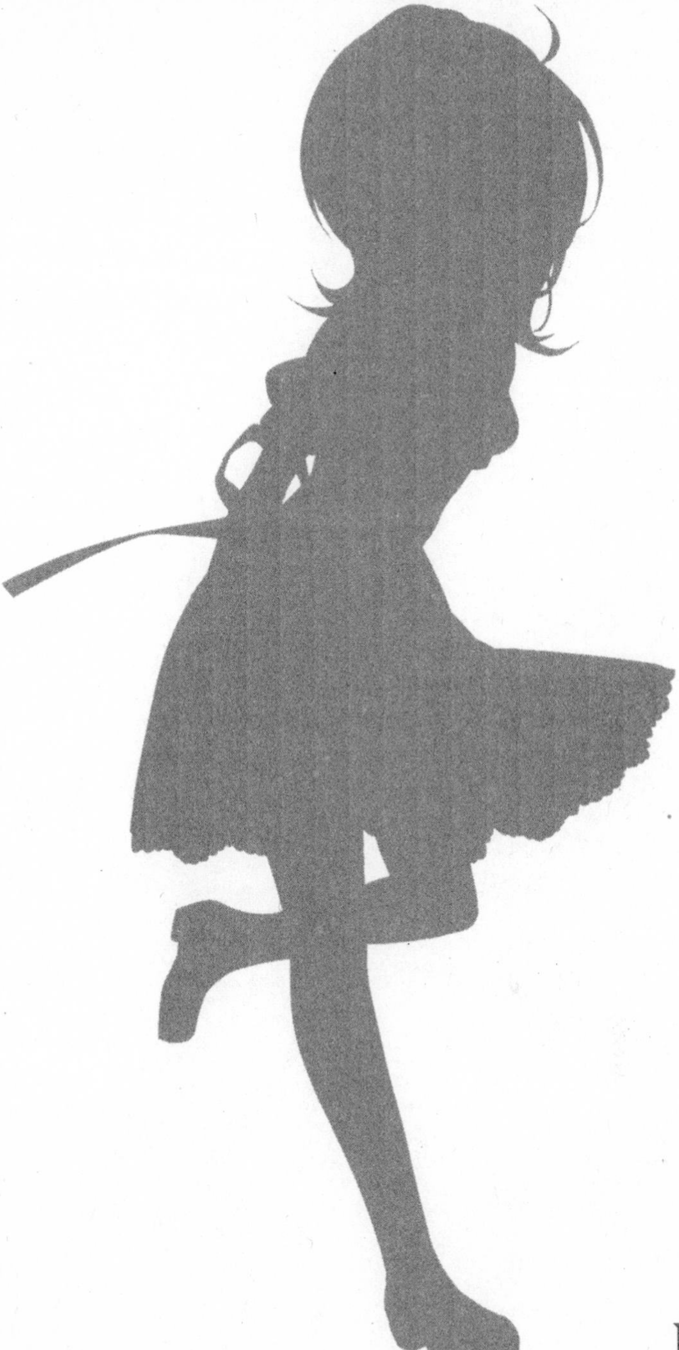

Intro

"Yes, I know it's late. That's why I'm asking you— Where have you been?!"

Nagisa Akatsuki sat in the passenger's seat of an old car, holding a smartphone in her hand, displeasure obvious in her voice. However, the alarm in her tone was probably due to the weak signal.

The landscape visible through the front window was marked by a treacherous cliff and a narrow, winding mountain road.

It was a little past eight PM. The prefectural road was dark, the only light coming from the occasional lamppost, and there were no signs of other vehicles passing through.

"Huh? The hospital?! What the—?! Who's in the hospital?! Celes...ta? Who? Er... Those voices just now... Yukina and Kanon are both with you?! Hey, Kojou...?! Ah!"

When the call suddenly cut off, Nagisa glared at the smartphone's screen with her cheeks puffed out. She immediately tried to reconnect, but the text displayed on the screen read a heartless OUT OF RANGE. The car had entered a tunnel.

"Oh? Kojou brought that middle schooler over to our place?" asked Gajou Akatsuki in amusement as he gripped the steering wheel.

When he chuckled aloud, Nagisa glared sullenly at the side of her father's face and said, "That's right. Sheesh, stupid Kojou! And here I was worried because I couldn't get through since yesterday!"

"Well, I'm sure a lot happened on the brat's end. Seems he had a scary chick from the CSA come visit and all."

"A chick?! What the—?! I can't believe it. This can't be happening. The minute I take my eyes off him, this happens…!" Nagisa murmured, sulking after Gajou's comment.

Gajou narrowed his eyes as he gazed at the side of his beloved daughter's upset face. He gave the car a little extra gas.

He hummed to a tune on the radio, which was a pop group's most recent song to hit the airwaves. The lyrics spoke frivolously of love and romance, and they did not suit him, a man dressed like some mafia gangster born a century too late, in the slightest. However, he didn't seem too concerned about his appearance.

Gajou and Nagisa were on their way to Kamioda District—a little village in the Tanzawa Mountains on the western edge of Kanagawa Prefecture—a peninsula surrounded by a lake.

This lake, known as Kannawa Lake, was a giant manmade body of water produced through the construction of a dam. It doubled as a bustling tourist attraction popular with fishermen and hikers.

The dam-created lake overlooked an old temple quietly constructed in the Tangiwa Mountains, away from prying eyes.

It was an odd shrine, and it was far from certain whether it was officially designated as a temple. The chief priest in charge of the priestesses therein was Hisano Akatsuki, Gajou's mother, and consequently, Nagisa's grandmother. He and Nagisa had traveled all the way from Itogami Island to see her.

"Took more time than I figured. Wonder if that old hag is still alive," Gajou murmured as he drove the car to the temple at the foot of the mountain.

From there, they'd have to walk up a long series of stone steps that ran all the way to the main building of the temple grounds.

"Gajou, you didn't call Granny to tell her we'd be arriving late? Is that okay? She's not going to be angry, right…?"

"It's fine. You get more patient as you get older, so she can cool her heels a bit. Besides, I'm gonna tell her we arrived late because *you* said you wanted to go shopping in Tokyo."

"Huhhh?! Wait, you're saying it's *my* fault?! You're the one who whined about needing to go to Dreamland and have lots of fun, Gajou!!"

"N-nah, that was just Daddy doing a favor for the family, y'see."

Gajou opened the driver's side door and got out of the car as if fleeing the scene. Then, when he looked up toward the temple's archway, his brows knotted in discomfort.

"Good grief... Things just ain't goin' my way."

"What?"

"Nagisa, sorry, could you wait here for a little bit?"

"Whaaa? Here? By myself?" Nagisa surveyed the surrounding darkness as a forlorn expression came over her. "I don't wanna. It's dark, it's cold, and I can't get a cell signal."

"Yeah, but having you climb stone stairs with your bags is a bit too much, ain't it? I'll call someone over. Hey, I'll lend you some handheld games."

"Geez, I'll pass. You wouldn't have anything but pervy dating sims and strip mah-jongg."

"Nonsense! I've also got a fighting game with state-of-the-art jiggle physics for the ladies. All the DLC outfits are unlocked, too."

"That's even worse!"

Nagisa stayed in the car with a look of dissatisfaction while Gajou headed toward the temple carrying a Boston bag in one hand.

It was the middle of winter, and there was too much snow falling for him to see the moon. However, Gajou's steps were confident as he climbed up the long stone stairway.

Kamioda Temple was virtually unknown to the public, but it had a long history deeply entwined with sorcery. Hisano, the chief cleric, was apparently involved in suppressing large-scale magical disasters several times over, and her ties to sorcerous governmental agencies did not run shallow by any means.

For that reason, Hisano had many guests visiting her around the start of the New Year. There were also worshippers native to the area, so Hisano and the priestesses ought to have been ready to receive guests during the season.

However, when Gajou arrived at the Kamioda Temple grounds, it was quiet—as still as the grave.

The lights were out in the main building and the clerical office. He did not detect any signs of people nearby.

Thanks to the grove of trees surrounding the area, it was pitch-black within the grounds, making him feel surrounded by complete darkness. Gajou stopped walking, unamused as he exhaled dramatically.

"Looks like I was right to leave Nagisa in the car... Come on out, already."

Gajou stuck his right hand into his coat pocket as he called out into the darkness, but no one answered. Even so, he was certain that humans had concealed themselves within the grounds. It was a projection of ill-intent too faint to call an aura. It included a tingle and a sense that there was a burning stench mingling with the air. It was a feeling he'd picked up on battlefields across the world: bloodlust from his enemies.

He snorted, grinning ferociously as he threw the grenade in his right hand without warning.

It exploded on the near side of a stone lantern some fourteen or fifteen meters away, kicking up an incredible blast of wind.

It was a stick-shaped hand grenade intended to neutralize an enemy through the explosive's concussive blast. Compared to a frag grenade, the lethal radius was rather small, but its power at point-blank range was high. The shock wave from the blast toppled the stone lantern, sending it tumbling down onto the figure hiding behind it.

Gajou's weapon changed what should have been cover into a weapon. There should not have been any time to get out of the way. But the fragment of the stone lantern that should have squashed the enemy flat flew against the shock wave of the explosion as it fell to the ground. It had fallen unnaturally, almost as if it had struck an invisible wall.

The hidden foe emerged, seemingly slicing through the rising cloud of dust.

It was a young girl in a school uniform. With both hands, she wielded a long, silver-colored, fully metallic sword.

"What the—?!"

Gajou grabbed a submachine gun from his bag and opened fire. It was loaded with rubber bullets, but it was a vicious weapon, certain to knock over anyone taking a square hit. However, the rounds bounced away from the girl right before her eyes. She'd created an invisible wall with a single flash of her long sword.

"Pseudo-spatial severing?! Der Freischötz...no, Rosen Chevalier Plus?!"

The instant Gajou's barrage relented, the sword-wielding girl closed the distance between them.

The girl's sword was a powerful holy weapon able to emulate the effects of a spell and sever space itself. The severed space in the wake of her blade functioned as a shield that could block any physical attack. Furthermore, the space-severing cuts of her sword could slice matter apart. Gajou's submachine gun could not fend off the girl's sword strikes. Trying would only result in the destruction of his firearm.

However, Rosen Chevalier Plus had weaknesses, too.

Gajou's right hand kept its grip on the submachine gun while his free left hand tossed a new hand grenade. This one sailed over the girl's head and exploded behind her.

"Urk!"

The girl turned her back on Gajou, swinging her long sword to slice the empty air.

Rosen Chevalier Plus's spatial severing effect lasted only for an instant, and furthermore, in a single direction only. The girl had been forced to turn her back on Gajou to protect herself from the grenade's blast.

Gajou trained the barrel of his submachine gun toward her wide-open back.

However, before he could squeeze the trigger, a blow struck his left hand. An arrow sailing through the darkness knocked Gajou's submachine gun from his grasp.

Another girl emerged, standing atop a sacred tree within the temple grounds. She was gripping a recurve bow that glowed silver. She had used the swordswoman as a decoy while she took aim at Gajou.

"Freikugel Plus...! This is bad. That thing can—!"

Gajou contorted his face out of anxiety. In the meantime, the girl had finished nocking a new arrow.

This second arrow launched without fanfare, releasing a high-pitched roar as it soared across the sky. The whistle attached to the arrow's tip created a spell incantation effect, activating a high-density curse. Freikugel Plus was no mere bow. It was a ritual-spell gun turret, able to spew curses anywhere within its range.

"Tch, a binding—"

Showered by the curse, Gajou's body was stiffening against his will.

This was a wide-area suppression ritual for neutralizing enemy infantry. Even Gajou never expected it to be used for the sake of a single person. His opponent cared not about appearances nor excess.

However, it wasn't impossible to counter—so long as you knew what made it tick.

Using his still-free right hand, Gajou narrowly managed to toss a new hand grenade overhead. This was a stun grenade, with no lethal force whatsoever.

An incredible flash of light tore through the night sky. The roar accompanying the blast shook the very air, creating a disturbance in the whistle arrow's high-density curse.

Almost simultaneously, Gajou's coat was enveloped in flames. The anti-spell charm woven into the coat's lining had activated. Magical symbols came to the surface of the smoking fabric, releasing Gajou from the binding spell's paralysis.

"A sonic magic circle from Freikugel Plus—broken by such a primitive method...!"

The sword-wielding girl's face twitched with shock as she rushed at Gajou with her blade. Gajou, still empty-handed, turned toward the girl, visibly annoyed as he curled up the corners of his lips.

"Sheesh, that's too dangerous for a brat like you to be swinging around. You need a spanking."

"Ah...?!"

When the girl tried to slice at him, Gajou dodged, slipping past her defenses.

The girl's defenseless flank was wide open to Gajou. A man of Gajou's close-combat skill ought to have been able to deliver a decisive blow that very instant. However, Gajou's hand slipped past her side, not touching the girl's body in any way.

"W-wait... Agh!"

Instantly, the girl spun around to pursue Gajou as he moved past, poising her sword once more. But a moment later, she went down like a ton of bricks. Something had entwined around the girl's legs, robbing her of her mobility.

That something was the girl's panties. As they had moved past one another, Gajou had pulled them down, tripping her up with her own underwear; she tumbled down on the spot.

"You bastard! How dare you do that to Yuiri—"

Standing up for the humiliated swordswoman, the archer moved to nock another arrow. However, before she could, Gajou pulled a new weapon out of the bag he'd dropped on the ground: a large-caliber, single-shot, break-action grenade launcher.

The girl readied her bow as Gajou looked her way and mercilessly fired a grenade at her.

The archer's expression did not shift as she aimed at the grenade in mid-flight. She meant to shoot the grenade out of the air. However, the grenade vigorously swelled in size before she could loose her arrow.

"Wha—?!"

The enlarged body of the grenade engulfed her. Its body turned out to be a highly adhesive, birdlime-like substance.

The bow-wielding girl, still poised to fall from the tree branch, had been glued upside-down to the trunk. She desperately attempted to hold down her skirt to prevent it from slipping up, but she was largely unable to move her body, thanks to the birdlime round's adhesiveness. Adorable yelps characteristic of her young age slipped out.

"Shio?!"

For an instant, the fallen sword-wielding girl paid attention to the plight of her birdlime-smeared comrade. Just as she did, Gajou blew a medical sprayer right in front of her nose. Attacked by powerful drowsiness, the girl could not even raise her voice as she collapsed and lost consciousness.

Checking that he'd completely put both out of commission, Gajou tossed the empty sprayer away.

"Sheesh. This is what happens when you give weapons to kids. Don't take it personally," he murmured apologetically.

He gazed at the long sword the girl had dropped. Gajou knew what the weapon truly was—and the name of the organization that had crafted it.

The temple had been empty, and these girls had attacked Gajou—those two facts were likely connected. The first thing he needed to do was question them and glean what information he could.

What a pain in the butt, Gajou thought, sighing as he approached the two girls. A moment later, Gajou heard a serene voice echoing from behind.

"You are in no position to look down on others, grasshopper."

"—?!"

Gajou felt a shudder course through his entire body as he drew a pistol from his pocket. The pistol fell to pieces while still in his hand.

"What the—?!"

"Too slow."

Gajou tried to look back, but his vision swayed. By the time he realized his chin had been struck, he'd been slammed into the ground.

"*Ka-ha!*" coughed Gajou, raggedly breathing out from his mouth. His limbs were too numb for him to make a move.

He did not even have time to gather his senses before someone drew close, pounding Gajou down with a bare hand. Even so, Gajou somehow managed to plant one knee on the ground and lift his face.

There were bright lights shining into Gajou's field of vision—lights from military pocket flashlights. Even at a single glance, the number of light sources exceeded twenty. Amid the backlight, a group emerged wearing camouflaged suits and armed with vicious-looking weapons. The firearm-wielding group of soldiers seemed to appear out of thin air, surrounding the temple grounds.

"That's crazy... Why are you...?!"

Gajou looked up at the person before him as he let out a painful groan.

The woman gazing down at Gajou with cold eyes was a silver-haired woman dressed in a *dougi*, a sleeveless outfit typically used for martial arts training. She gripped a wooden *naginata* in her right hand. And her left arm was wrapped around Nagisa, unconscious and asleep.

The camouflaged soldiers thrust their gun barrels toward Gajou, who was unable to rise to his feet. Even for him, resistance in this situation would be reckless. Gajou sluggishly raised both hands, looking up at the starless sky.

"…Well, ain't I shit outta luck."

Gajou sighed, his breath visible against the cold air, as he murmured to himself.

Thus Gajou Akatsuki's homecoming began in the absolute worst way he could imagine.

CHAPTER ONE
COUNTDOWN TO
THE NEW YEAR

1

With direct sunlight pouring in, the deserted corridor shimmered like a mirage.

From the open window, a muggy wind blew into the classroom.

Sitting alone in the seat directly across from the teacher's desk, Kojou Akatsuki wore a forlorn expression as he struggled with a difficult text written in English. Large droplets of sweat rolled incessantly down his forehead. It was depressing how his moist wrist stuck to the answer sheet.

"So hot…"

Kojou let out a frail murmur as he tugged at the collar of his uniform.

The clear blue sky spread outside the window seemed straight out of midsummer. A cumulonimbus cloud hovered over a corner of the horizon, and the chirping cicadas were noisily out of season.

Somehow managing to solve the last problem, Kojou put down his mechanical pencil—also slick with sweat—and said, "Hey, Natsuki. You know, today's—"

Before he could finish, something like an invisible fist smacked him between the eyes, scattering pale sparks all about. Natsuki Minamiya, standing at the teacher's podium, cruelly watched Kojou as he recoiled backward.

"Fool. Do not address your homeroom teacher by her first name when she's already in a bad mood from this terrible heat."

"That's no reason for a teacher to use violence on a student, is it…?!"

Kojou put a hand on his forehead as he retorted, grimacing with tearful eyes. Natsuki, sitting on an extravagant, antique chair, coldly snorted and strangled Kojou's objection with silence.

"Aaaaaaaaaaaaaaah."

For some reason, the homunculus girl wearing a maid outfit was mimicking a voice recital as she sat in front of an electric fan next to Natsuki. Kojou hadn't seen the electric fan before, but apparently, she'd taken quite a deep interest in it. As a result, Astarte was completely monopolizing the fan, but since she'd brought it in from the staff room in the first place, Kojou was in no position to complain.

"...Today's New Year's Eve, yeah?"

"Indeed, it is. The New Year will arrive in little over half a day."

Natsuki bluntly replied to Kojou's half-hearted question. Halfway through listening to her response, Kojou stuck his chin on his palm and said:

"Why do I have to cram in extra lessons right at the end of the year like this?"

"Because some idiot with too many unapproved absences and too many red marks on supplementary tests in my subject *asked* for them. Astarte, help me out a little."

"Accepted."

At Natsuki's command, the homunculus girl went out of her way to retrieve a mirror and place it in front of Kojou. For a time, he silently gazed at his reflection.

Then he cried out, "Wait, this is sarcasm!"

He shooed Astarte away. The homunculus girl in the maid outfit returned to her seat in front of the electric fan.

Natsuki sipped on the tasty tropical iced tea she'd had Astarte make for her. "If you have time to ask pointless questions, why don't you thank me a little for putting up with extra lessons even on a day like this?"

"Ah well, yeah, I'm grateful for that. Seriously." Kojou politely bowed his head as he handed the short answer sheet to Natsuki.

Eight months had passed since Kojou inherited the power of the World's Mightiest Vampire. Thereafter, Kojou's allowed absences had whittled away in the course of becoming wrapped up in one troublesome incident after another. If Natsuki hadn't spent her precious extended

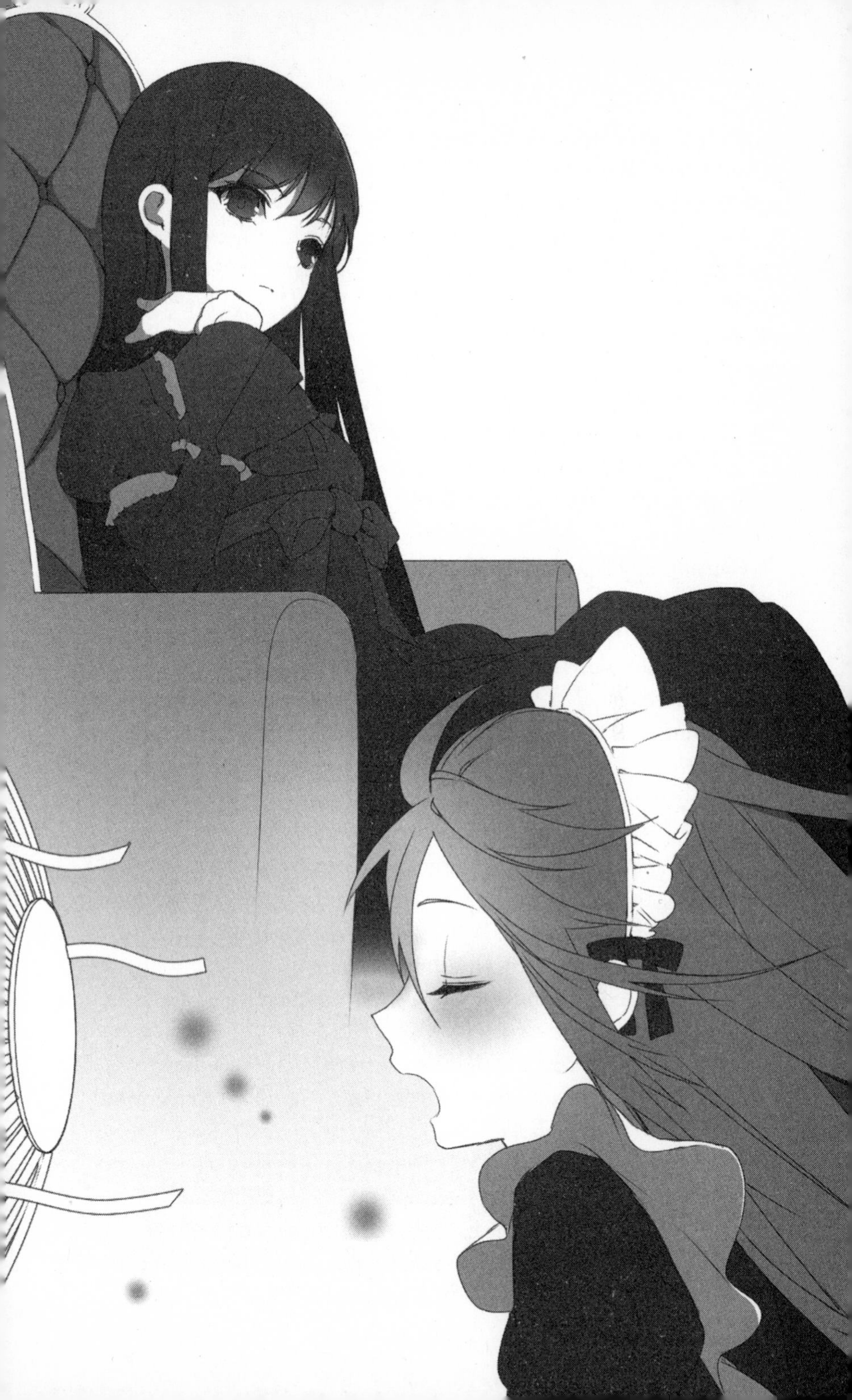

vacation giving him these extra lessons, Kojou would be dead set to repeat the year by that point.

"Hmph."

However, Natsuki was slightly taken aback, perhaps not really believing Kojou would voice his gratitude so easily, when she twisted her lips and said:

"Well, fine. Incidentally, Kojou, where is your father right now?"

"…Huh?"

At Natsuki's sudden question, it was Kojou's turn to get suspicious.

Kojou's father, Gajou Akatsuki, was an archeologist. Due to the nature of his work, he spent most of the year overseas, rarely returning to Itogami Island. Of course, that left few opportunities to come into contact with Natsuki.

"Natsuki, why do you know about h…? Wait, don't tell me…"

The first word to emerge in the back of Kojou's mind was *adultery*. Natsuki might have looked like a little girl, but apparently, she was twenty-six years old. That meant she was more than old enough to have an old flame or two.

But the moment those thoughts came to mind, Natsuki violently pinched Kojou's cheek and said, "Those are the eyes of a man picturing something quite rude, Kojou Akatsuki."

"Ow! Ow! —Hey, I didn't even say anything yet!!"

"Enough about that. Answer the question already."

"He's not on Itogami Island right now. He took my little sister and went off to Grandma's place in Tanzawa!" Kojou blurted out while he sustained Natsuki's merciless punishment.

Natsuki let out a "Hmm" and slackened her grip on Kojou as she sank into thought.

"So for once, that man actually told the truth about something…"

"How the heck do you know him anyway, Natsuki?" Kojou asked, putting a hand on his aching cheek.

Natsuki gave an annoyed sigh as she replied, "I know Gajou Akatsuki from his numerous unwelcome interruptions in my side business. Well, I do grudgingly concede that he has been useful on very rare occasions…"

"Your side business…? What the heck's that shitty dad of mine been up to…?" Kojou muttered. A bad feeling came over him.

Natsuki was a teacher, but her side business was as a federal Attack Mage with the right to capture sorcerous criminals. Educational facilities within a Demon Sanctuary were required to have a certain proportion of staff on hand with Attack Mage certification. Therefore, an Attack Mage doubling as a teacher was by no means rare. In point of fact, Saikai Academy had one for each grade; in other words, it employed five additional Attack Mages as teachers in addition to Natsuki.

However, Natsuki occupied a special role that set her apart from her peers, for her might as an Attack Mage was so exceptional that she continued to aid active criminal investigations.

Therefore, Gajou had come into contact with Natsuki in the course of *that* business. In other words, Gajou was on the scene where sorcerous crimes were taking place. Kojou couldn't help but be concerned about that.

"Can you get in touch with Gajou Akatsuki?"

Natsuki continued her line of questioning, paying Kojou's unease no heed.

"That might be a little tough. Cell phone signals don't reach that area, y'see."

Kojou didn't know Gajou's cell phone number in the first place, but he kept quiet about that.

"The place your grandmother lives in is quite the backwoods, then?" she asked with a serious tone.

"Pretty much, yeah." He gave a heavy nod.

"So what is this all of a sudden? You need to talk to him 'bout something?"

"No… There was just a little something on my mind," she replied vaguely, not helping his current doubts.

He shuddered involuntarily as he said, "Hey—cut that out. Now you're making *me* worried. I already told you Nagisa's with him and everything."

"Nagisa Akatsuki… You did say something like that, didn't you…?"

Natsuki's brows furled, as if she liked how things were unfolding less and less. Her murmur alarmed him further. It seemed Natsuki really had come into contact with Gajou in the recent past.

Maybe it really is adultery. When Kojou seriously entertained the suspicion, Natsuki suddenly glared at him with half-lidded eyes.

"Well, setting all that aside, Kojou Akatsuki, what is with this score?"

"Huh? Did I completely bomb it?"

A perplexed expression came over Kojou as she thrust the marked answer sheet toward his face. The number written in red pencil was sixty-six out of one hundred—not a great score, but not terrible, either.

"I can hardly believe you achieved a score this high through your own ability. You couldn't possibly have slipped some cheating method past my supervision, could you…?"

Natsuki spoke these words while staring at Kojou in utter seriousness.

"Umm, no way this score is high enough to suspect cheating, and even I can do this well if I study hard, y'know."

Kojou, fully understanding the reason for Natsuki's doubts, desperately tried to refute them. Compared to his previous tests, chock-full of red marks, you'd think this one was so good that it came from a different person, but no casual observer would consider that score to be worthy of praise. They were the grades of a student dead set to repeat a year. The fact that this kind of score was enough to make her suspect cheating was a harsh blow to Kojou's pride.

But he could understand Natsuki's feeling of surprise. Since becoming a vampire, Kojou had no time to study—a situation that hadn't really changed.

"To think you would actually study for extra lessons. What's gotten into you?"

"Umm, I just thought that, well, you know… I really should take my classes more seriously…"

For the one who can't take them at all, Kojou continued to himself.

For an instant, the side of a blonde girl's face, always making a small, trembling smile, flashed before his eyes.

Avrora Florestina. The twelfth Kaleid Blood.

Ever since he'd regained fragments of his memories of her, Kojou's mental state had undergone subtle changes that even he didn't understand. That didn't mean the situation he was placed in had changed very much, but when he thought about what he could do, he thought he could at least put in the effort on short tests, but—

"It's not like an education has any downsides. Besides, gotta think about the future, right?" Kojou said earnestly, almost saying it just for his own sake.

To be blunt, he still had little appreciation for his status, but in name, at least, Kojou was the vampire known as the Fourth Primogenitor; furthermore, vampire primogenitors were granted a life span that was nigh eternal.

The issue causing Kojou a much greater deal of concern was picking a career.

Even vampires needed to put food on the table, and clothes and a place to stay required money. If one was born a commoner and not an aristocrat, they worked, or they starved. He wasn't like Dimitrie Vattler or Giada Kukulkan, both possessing vast territories. All that said, he didn't think the stupid title of *World's Mightiest Vampire* was worth much on a résumé.

And so, having agonized over the matter, Kojou made an honest attempt at getting an education. Surely, academic knowledge had no downside for an undying, ageless vampire; if it qualified him for gainful employment and let him get his hands on a trade, all the better.

Kojou hadn't actually intended to explain things to Natsuki that far. If some other vampire primogenitor said *I'd better study seriously, so I don't go hungry down the road*, Kojou would make fun of him, too.

"I see."

However, Natsuki flashed a charming smile, almost as though she could see right through to Kojou's feelings. This was not her usual smile, the cold one that made her seem like she was looking down on the entire world. This was a gentle smile, the sort one gave to a younger brother. Natsuki's soft expression, one Kojou was seeing for the first time, made it hard to pay attention to anything else.

"…Natsuki?"

When Kojou murmured without thinking, Natsuki silently delivered a sharp blow to his forehead. In the meantime, the beautiful, charming smile from before had vanished like an illusion.

"Well, fine. I suppose I will give you a passing grade for today's lesson."

"Thanks a bunch."

"Do try to greet the New Year on good terms."

"Gotcha."

Kojou lobbed his curt reply as he pressed a hand to his stinging forehead. Natsuki returned to the armchair, elegantly sipping her iced tea. Just as before, Astarte was sitting reverentially before the electric fan, saying "Weee aaare..." like some kind of alien from outer space.

Then, when Kojou, who felt a brief sense of liberation, tidied up the writing supplies and gently opened the classroom door, a new person emerged. This was Misaki Sasasaki, the physical education teacher.

"All done?"

Dressed in sporty attire, the female teacher confirmed with Natsuki that the lesson was done before she shifted her gaze to Kojou, who stood frozen in place. Of course, Kojou's egregious number of absences meant English was by no means the only subject he needed extra classes in.

"Sorry to spoil things when you've neatly wrapped up, but after English is gym. We're doing a ten-kilometer marathon, so get changed and meet me out on the grounds, 'kay?"

Misaki smiled at Kojou as she spoke in her oddly tense tone.

Kojou stared at the brightly glimmering midday sun; then he shifted his eyes to the sports field scorched by its rays. Itogami Island, floating in the middle of the Pacific Ocean, was an island of eternal summer with a tropical climate. Even on New Year's Eve, the temperature close to noon was butting against 30 degrees Celsius.

And Kojou was a vampire, weak to direct sunlight.

"...Seriously?"

A frail murmur escaped Kojou's mouth as the fear of impending death coursed through him.

Astarte's serene voice echoed toward the electric fan as it was seemingly sucked into the blue sky.

2

Kojou, finally freed from his lessons some two-odd hours later, headed toward the monorail with a wobbly gait.

Walking beside him was Yukina Himeragi, carrying a black guitar case on her back. She'd been waiting the whole time for Kojou to finish his lessons so she could resume her duty as watcher of the Fourth Primogenitor.

"Umm... Are you all right, senpai?"

Concerned, Yukina looked up at the hollow expression on Kojou's face.

"Yeah, somehow... Jeez, I seriously thought I was gonna shrivel up like a prune..."

Kojou shook his head violently, apparently to get his head back in the game, and formed a smile with no strength behind it. Thanks to overusing his brain cells on the test and walking what seemed like a ten-kilometer marathon beneath the scorching sun, Kojou was completely and utterly drained. Both mind and body were at their limits. The road to the station was less than a fifteen-minute walk, but it felt impossibly far.

"First, please rehydrate. Then, have this. It's a lemon dipped in honey."

"Ahh, thanks."

Appreciative of the ever-reliable Yukina, Kojou accepted the sports drink and the lemon.

Technically, Kojou was the World's Mightiest Vampire, and Yukina was Kojou's watcher, dispatched by the Japanese government. However, no one looking at them that moment was likely to believe that. They looked like nothing more than an athletics club member right after a match and his shrewd, quick-witted manager.

"Sorry for making you come with me to school on New Year's Eve like this, Himeragi."

As soon as he recovered a bit of stamina, Kojou expressed his appreciation to Yukina all over again. Kojou hadn't asked for Yukina to follow him around, but it was a simple fact that she'd helped with lots of things.

"It is no trouble at all. After all, it is my mission to watch you, senpai," she replied with her usual all-business expression.

Kojou unwittingly made a pained smile at Yukina's stereotypical reply as he said, "Somehow, this takes me back to right after I met you, Himeragi."

"Oh...?"

Yukina's face stiffened, seemingly put on guard by Kojou's sudden declaration. She pressed a hand to the hem of her skirt, inching backward as if to avoid his gaze.

"Wh...what are you remembering?! Did I not ask you to forget about that?!"

"…Huh?! Ah!"

Kojou panicked as he saw the explosion of redness on Yukina's cheeks. He remembered that in the place he'd first bumped into Yukina, he had seen her panties—not once, but twice in quick succession. It was a most unfortunate accident upon their first meeting.

"No! Not that time!"

"Which is 'this' time and which is the 'other' time?!"

"I meant school! I met you when I was heading to school for extra lessons, right, Himeragi?"

"…I suppose so, now that you mention it…"

Yukina finally lowered her guard somewhat. The first time Kojou and Yukina had a chance to properly speak to each other was the day after that first encounter. It was right before the end of summer vacation. That day, too, Kojou was heading to school by himself to receive extra lessons, whereupon Yukina, a transfer student at the middle school, appeared before him.

"Back then, I had just about the worst possible impression of you, though—the way you turned your spear on me for no good reason."

"I—I believe you were responsible for that, senpai! I believe that was very much the case!"

For once, Yukina was flustered in her response. Apparently, Yukina's impulsive behavior at the time was an embarrassing memory she did not particularly want to remember.

"I mean, even though they told me you were the World's Mightiest Vampire, you seemed oddly flaky. I could not really tell what you were up to, the talk of memory loss seemed very fishy, and you were indecent… How could I possibly trust a person like that?!"

"I wasn't indecent! Seeing your panties back then was totally an act of God!"

"I told you to forget about that!"

Yukina walked toward the station at a rapid pace, leaving Kojou behind. He lowered his shoulders in exasperation and chased after her.

Even when they boarded the monorail, Yukina kept her face turned away from him as if she was sulking. Left with no avenues to pursue, Kojou pulled out his cell phone and began quietly checking his messages.

The interior of the monorail car was emptier than usual, no doubt because few people commuted on New Year's Eve. The jovial atmosphere despite that was probably because it was the year's end, too. Even the billboard in the car was plastered with New Year's greetings and advertisements for New Year's sales.

"Senpai… Umm, about our conversation earlier…"

It was a while after the monorail set out that Yukina hesitantly opened her mouth. Kojou was still looking at his cell phone when he replied in a tone that seemed absentminded somehow.

"Mm? Ahh, you mean about the panti—"

"Not that!"

The plastic strap Yukina was holding audibly creaked under the power of her grip.

"I said earlier that I could not trust you, senpai…b-but I do not feel that way about you anymore, so…"

Yukina's voice was tense, as if she had wrenched considerable courage out of herself. She must have been quietly dwelling on how she'd unintentionally scolded Kojou out of stubbornness.

"Ah…yeah."

"I mean, you are certainly as unreliable as before, sloppy, not self-aware of your being a Primogenitor, you get far too comfortable with other girls as soon as I take my eyes off you, and your incorrigible indecency is not a good thing, in my opinion, but you do still possess a few admirable qualities…"

"Uh-huh."

"And I thought I should tell you that I do understand this, senpai, having watched you for these past four months."

"Mm."

Kojou had yet to meet Yukina's gaze as she continued to explain herself, her voice threatening to fade away. However, Kojou's reaction was indifferent. He showed no particular sign of satisfaction as he let Yukina's words roll past him.

"…Um, er… Senpai, are you listening?"

Naturally, Yukina lifted her face and looked up at Kojou, sensing that something was off. Kojou, gazing vacantly at his cell phone, blinked in mild surprise and asked:

"Huh? Ah, sorry. What'd you say?"

"Senpai…!"

Yukina scowled irritably when she realized that Kojou hadn't listened to a word she'd said.

"S-sorry about that. Nagisa hasn't been in touch for a while, so that was kinda on my mind…"

"Haaa…" Yukina glared at Kojou and let out a deep sigh as he hastily tried to vindicate himself. "A while, you say… You were able to call her normally up to last week, yes?"

"Yeah, but it's been a whole week since then. She said she was just about to arrive at Grandma's place, and I haven't gotten one word from her since, so that's kinda worrying me a bit."

"Didn't you tell me that cell phone signals do not reach where Nagisa went for the New Year? If so, I would think there is nothing unnatural about that being the case…"

"Well, yeah."

Kojou grudgingly agreed with Yukina's exceedingly sensible assertion. Now that his inbox was empty, he checked his missed calls one last time before putting his cell phone back in his pocket.

"Besides, Grandma works people pretty hard. I think she's probably just too busy helping at the temple to send me a message."

"Then, there is no need to be so concerned."

"Yeah…"

Kojou nodded, unable to rebut her. Even he could understand that it was outside the social norm for a little sister in middle school to call her older brother without a good reason.

"Incidentally, Himeragi, what were you talking about earlier?"

Having apparently recovered his senses, Kojou looked straight at Yukina.

"Eh…?! Ah, umm, nothing at all."

Startled, Yukina's entire body went rigid before she shook her head in manic protest. Apparently, he was directly asking about a subject that contained details that were difficult to voice out loud.

"Hmmm."

Displaying no particular interest, Kojou did not pry further, readily dropping the subject. As he did, Yukina glared at the side of his face, murmuring:

"Stupid senpai…!"

3

Kojou ate a quick lunch in front of the station, and by the time he arrived back home, it was a little past three. Less than nine hours remained before the year was over.

Taking the elevator to the apartment building's seventh floor, Kojou opened the door to his own apartment, room 704. "Pardon me," said Yukina quietly, following Kojou into the entryway.

About ten days earlier, an incident had occurred that had left Yukina's room—room 705—a complete disaster, and while repairs were technically complete, it still lacked the furniture and appliances required for everyday living. Thus, due to circumstances beyond her control, Yukina had become something like a houseguest at Kojou's place.

A third party would invariably mistake the situation for cohabitation, but Yukina had stated that she needed to keep Kojou under even stricter observation. Because this eased the burdens of living at home alone, Kojou had no compelling reason to drive her out, either.

Having thus entered the apartment together without any particular misgivings, Yukina and Kojou both gasped in shock—for the three-bedroom apartment was in a state of total chaos. Everything in the drawers had been dumped onto the floor; the closet doors were open, too.

"What the hell?!"

"Don't tell me…a burglar?!"

Sensing a human presence, Yukina stepped ahead to shield Kojou. Apparently, the intruder who had made a mess of the apartment was still present.

Kojou followed Yukina's vigilant gaze when he, too, discerned the intruder's location: the near side of the corridor in the master bedroom, usually left closed and unused.

Yukina, seemingly on guard in case the opponent was armed, cautiously opened the door. Then they laid eyes upon an individual wearing a frumpy white coat, sitting on the edge of the bed.

She was probably around thirty, give or take. She had unkempt, disheveled hair and eyes that seemed reluctant to open all the way. At first glance, the young-faced woman came off as a negligent adult.

She heaved a contemplative sigh as she noticed Kojou and Yukina entering the room, adding, "Wow, Kojou. And Yukina, too. Perfect timing!"

"Gah…"

"Miss Mimori?"

Kojou let out a low groan as a surprised Yukina addressed her by name.

Sitting on the side of the bed and rummaging through the closet was none other than Mimori Akatsuki—Kojou's mother. She usually slept at her workplace, more because she found commuting to be a pain than anything else, normally returning home once every week or so. But apparently, her colleagues had managed to shoo her out of the lab for New Year's.

That said, Mimori was the rightful occupant of the apartment. Of course, Kojou and Yukina had a hard time understanding why Mimori would turn her own apartment into a cluttered bird's nest.

She reached for a piece of luggage at the back of the closet and explained, "I finally found my suitcase, but there are things in the way, so I couldn't get it out. Hold it down for a sec, would you?"

"W-wait!"

Kojou hastily tried to stop Mimori as she grabbed hold of the suitcase handle and gave it a good, hard yank.

For Mimori, who lacked any domestic capabilities whatsoever, the term "messy adult" did not even begin to accurately describe her. The closet in her room was packed with all sorts of things. The contents had less space between them than a wood mosaic.

It was painfully easy to guess what would happen when the suitcase was yanked out. However, despite Kojou's valiant efforts to prevent the inevitable, the wall of luggage collapsed, causing a wave of clutter to crash down onto him.

"What a relief. Now I can finally pack."

Mimori, the culprit of that tragic spectacle, opened her suitcase in good humor, ignorant of her son's suffering. Thanks to Kojou's body acting as a dam, she escaped the luggage landslide unscathed.

"You see all this, and that's all you have to say…?"

Kojou, bruised all over, pointed to the luggage scattered on the floor as he chided his mother. However, his words simply mystified her.

"Well, there's no time. Tonight, I'm heading out for the company trip to Hokkaido."

"You never mentioned that to me!"

"Oh, did you want to go, Kojou?"

"Nah, I'll pass. I went through hell when I went with you on that company trip when I was in middle school!"

"Did you, now?"

"How could you forget?! I lost all my clothes in strip ping-pong, I lost all my New Year's money betting in mah-jongg... All sorts of stuff happened!"

Kojou's eyes glazed over as he recalled the bitter experience. Mimori let his grumbling wash over her like she was listening to background music at a coffee shop.

"Incidentally, I don't see Nagisa anywhere... Kojou, do you know where she is?"

"Dad took Nagisa to go see Grandma in Tangiwa. —A week ago."

Notice faster, dammit, went Kojou, sighing with an exasperated look.

The instant Mimori heard the words *Grandma in Tangiwa*, her expression heavily contorted, almost as if by reflex. For Mimori, one to take everything in stride, it was a rare look of dismay.

"Tch... That ghastly old bag is still alive?"

"Gh...ghastly old bag?"

A bewildered look came over Yukina as she watched Mimori curse her elder with vivid enmity.

Kojou whispered to Yukina, "Mom and Grandma don't get along very well."

Yukina gave a bewildered nod of understanding. One was an airheaded psychic working as a researcher for an international conglomerate; the other was a rogue Attack Mage and spiritualist working as a priestess at a shrine. They had no common ground to speak of, and beyond being a wife and a mother-in-law, their mutual compatibility was abysmal. Small wonder Gajou hadn't said a word to Mimori about that year's homecoming.

"More importantly, why is this house so messy? Don't tell me this is all from looking for that suitcase...?" Kojou inquired as he surveyed the area.

Mimori seemed to notice the dismal state of the apartment for the first time. Gazing at the luggage strewn about the floor, she looked surprised for a moment as she said:

"Oh, th-this is—you see... Yes, end-of-the-year cleaning!"

"...Huh?"

"Doesn't it feel really good to get rid of a year's worth of grime on New Year's Eve and face the New Year with a clean slate?"

"D-don't make up such convenient lies! You made that up just now, didn't you?!"

Kojou responded a moment late to Mimori's all-too-innocent explanation. While he tried to regain his footing, Mimori smiled in victory and changed topics.

"Mm-hmm... Well, never mind that. The two of you, stand side by side. Yes, right over there."

"Ah...?"

Prodded by Mimori to stand near the window, Kojou did as instructed, largely on reflex.

"Yes, Yukina, can you take one step closer to Kojou?"

"L-like this?"

Yukina stood right beside Kojou, still unable to grasp what was going on.

Mimori, seeing that Kojou and Yukina were nestled right against each other, suddenly said in a completely serious voice, "Now, question. What is Napier's constant e's logarithm to the second power?"

What the heck? Kojou froze, not understand his mother's question in the slightest. He couldn't even tell if she was speaking Japanese anymore.

For her part, Yukina looked just as bewildered as she easily solved the problem, resulting in...

"Two...?"

Yukina tilted her head as she brought up the index and middle fingers of her right hand.

And because the Japanese word for two is *ni*, Yukina's expression broke into a little smile. Mimori did not let the instant slip by, quickly snapping the shutter of the digital camera she'd brought out.

As a result, she had taken a commemorative photo recording Kojou

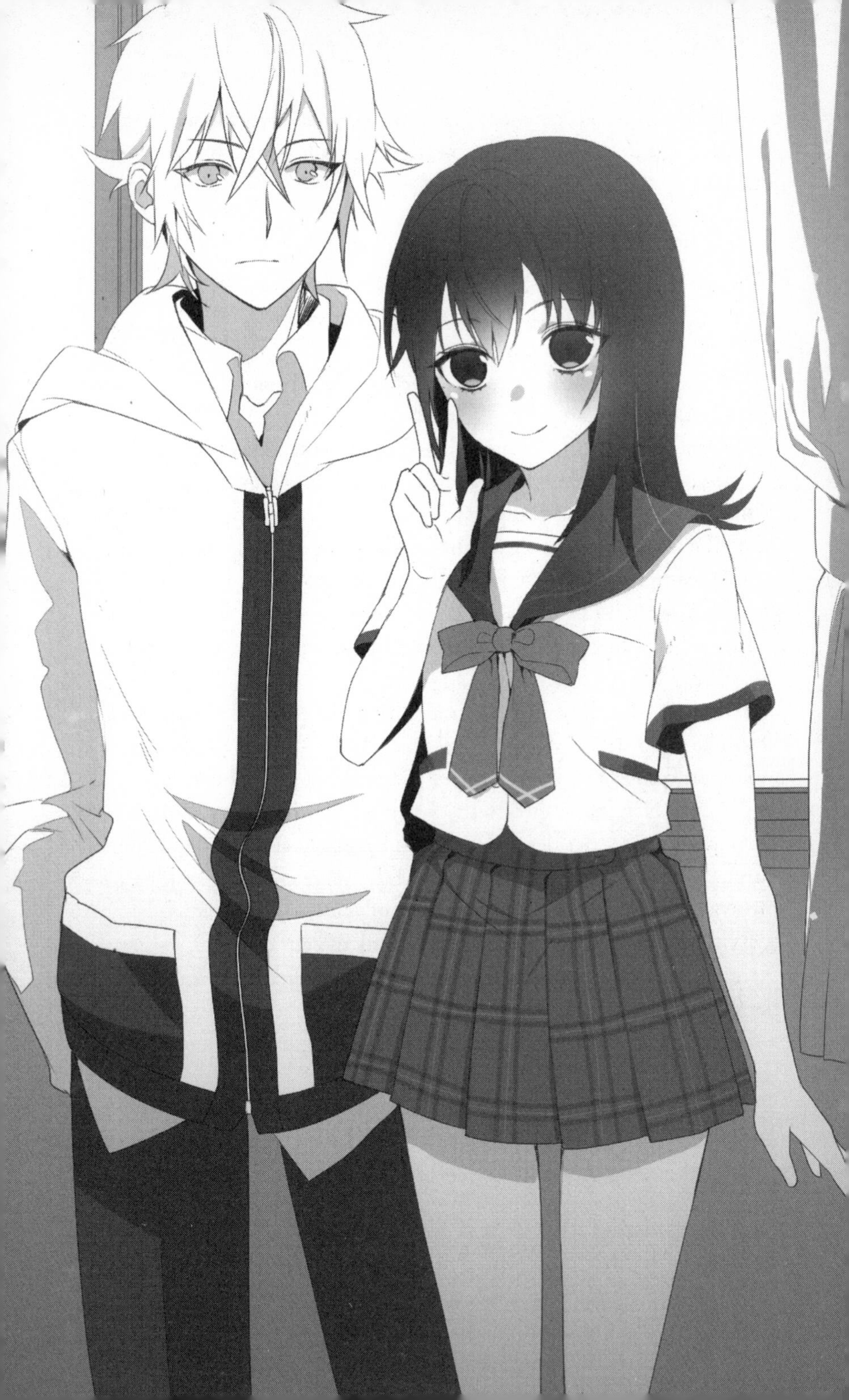

and Yukina in an intimate-looking scene. Furthermore, the way Yukina was making a peace sign with a smiling face made it a frighteningly rare image.

"Er, umm..."

"Mm. That came out pretty well."

In contrast to Yukina, unable to conceal her distress, Mimori smiled, satisfied. Kojou glared at his mother with a sharp look.

"What the heck are you up to...?"

"Alrighty. Yukina, I'll give this camera to you. I found it when I was cleaning the room earlier."

"You mean you stuffed it in the closet by mistake, don't you?"

Kojou's harsh jab didn't even elicit a twitch from Mimori.

Yukina accepted the compact, digital camera and its metallic silver case. The device was no bigger than a small smartphone model, yet its lens was very large. From all appearances, it was an expensive, state-of-the-art camera.

The camera's manufacturer was MAR—the international conglomerate Mimori worked for.

"Is it really all right to give me something like this...?" Yukina asked, bashful.

Mimori displayed a teasing smile. "It's fine, it's fine. Think of it as an impromptu New Year's gift. In the first place, it's a prototype from work that I got for free. Besides, if I give it to Kojou, he'll use it for nefarious purposes, like taking pictures of you while you're changing, taking pictures of your underwear, taking pictures of you in the shower..."

"Like hell I will! How poorly do you think of your own son?!"

Kojou made a show of his objection to being treated like some sort of peeping tom.

A small, knowing smile escaped Yukina. "If that is the alternative... thank you very much."

"Whaddaya mean *that*?" Kojou grumbled, twisting his lips in displeasure.

Mimori, seeing Yukina so reserved and happy, gently narrowed her eyes.

"Mm-hmm, human memories are surprisingly hazy, so it isn't so bad to make your memories tangible. Important moments that you don't realize you'll miss until you lose them…"

"Miss Mimori…?"

Yukina lifted her face, giving Mimori a look of deep respect. However, Mimori, a glutton for praise, got carried away as she said:

"Well, I'm a psychometer anyway, so I'm completely fine without photos at all, you know!"

"Like we need to hear that! What are you so proud of?!"

Kojou muttered, visibly annoyed by Mimori's childish behavior. Unsure whether or not Kojou and Mimori had a good mother-son relationship, Yukina couldn't help but giggle.

With a smile on her face, Mimori continued stuffing her suitcase full of things and closed the lid of the overflowing case with one hard push.

"Okay, packing complete. Kojou, I'll leave the rest to you."

"Hey! Wait—are you planning to run?!"

Naturally, when Kojou saw his mother darting across the cluttered apartment, he tried to stop her. However, when Kojou barred her path, Mimori sent him flying with the suitcase.

"H-Himeragi! Stop her!"

"Yukina, take care of Kojou in the New Year, 'kay?"

"Eh?! Ah, yes… *Eek!*"

Yukina jumped a little as Mimori, passing through, gave her butt a little pat. The opening allowed Mimori to slip past Yukina and charge out the front door, her sandals flopping around as she ran.

Dumbfounded and drained of strength, Kojou and Yukina watched the woman flee.

The damage Mimori had wrought did not stop with the bedroom. The living room, the kitchen, and even Kojou's and Nagisa's rooms had been ravaged in equal measure. It looked like a localized tornado had passed through. Putting everything back into its original state would require much more time and effort than the average cleaning.

"So…in the end, it's *my* job to clean this whole thing up?"

Kojou, sluggishly rising to his feet, felt a twinge of despair as he shook his head. As he did, Yukina stood beside him, fraily letting out a sigh.

"No, senpai. It's *our* job."

4

It took the two of them quite a while to clean up the wreckage inside the apartment. It was nine fifteen PM. Only two hours and forty-five minutes remained in the year.

Right after Kojou took a shower, finally washing off the sweat and dust, the doorbell rang. The monitor displayed the face of his friend Motoki Yaze, who was quickly becoming an eyesore.

"Heya, Kojou. I'm here."

Sporting a pair of earbuds around his neck, his spiky-haired classmate let himself into the apartment. He was holding a convenience store bag with both hands.

"What're you doing here at this time of day?"

Kojou narrowed his eyes as he toweled his damp hair and greeted his friend.

"What're you talkin' about?" Yaze, in apparent disappointment, continued, "We all promised to make the first temple visit of the year together, right? We were supposed to meet up at your place for it."

"Oh yeah…" Kojou nodded. "Guess we did."

Thanks to the extra lessons and the cleaning piled on top of that, the scheduled meet up had slipped right out of his mind. Plus, losing touch with Nagisa had done a number on Kojou's ability to concentrate.

"Come to think of it, what's got you all worn out, Kojou?"

"Ah…well, a bunch of stuff happened not too long ago."

"Ohhh?"

For some reason, Yaze's eyes glimmered in a show of heavy interest.

"Well, allow me to intrude. I just bought sweets and drinks, after all."

"Not that I mind but… Come to think of it, where are the others? Wasn't Asagi with you?"

"They should be here any moment, I think. There, see?"

At the same time Yaze pointed behind him, new figures appeared at the entrance. One was a female high school student with an extravagant hairstyle; the other was a small-statured elementary school girl. With unsteady, precarious-looking steps, they both somehow made it to the Akatsuki residence's front door. Kojou's eyes went wide at their luxurious outfits.

"What are you two doing in those getups...?" Kojou asked in a bewildered tone.

Normally, extravagant hair was Asagi's trademark, but this day, it felt even showier than usual. She wore a long-sleeved kimono with countless flowers scattered over thin, pale-scarlet fabric.

Led by the hand was Yume Eguchi, also wearing a long-sleeved kimono. Hers was made with a bright blue-green checkered fabric featuring a pattern that depicted a cute collection of treasures.

Either way, they were dazzling outfits most suited for greeting the New Year...were they not on an island of never-ending summer in the middle of the Pacific Ocean, that is.

"W...well, it's New Year's Eve, so I thought *Why not wear something really colorful for once?*"

"D-do they look good on us, Mister Kojou?"

After going to such lengths to get dressed up, Asagi and Yume were eager for words of praise. However, their smiling faces were hollow, and their eyes slightly out of focus. The excessive heat was robbing them of their senses.

"Oh, I was just thinking that long sleeves were a no go with this island's climate. You girls doing okay...?" he asked, concerned.

Asagi and Yume appeared wobbly and they weren't even sweating anymore—clear signs of impending heat exhaustion. Small wonder, given that they were walking around wearing long-sleeved layered kimonos as New Year's outfits on the tropical Itogami Island.

Even so, Yume put on a reassuring smile and said, "W-we'll be all right. As long as we drink plenty of water..."

"However, if you felt the need to lower the temperate on the air conditioner a little, I wouldn't complain," Asagi said as she lumbered into the living room and plopped down on the sofa.

Kojou sighed and adjusted things with the remote control. "Well fine, but you're sure you don't just wanna change clothes? I can loan you some."

"It's fine. We've made it this far, and we have our pride as women to consider."

"The first one to give in loses."

"Um, there's nothing competitive about the first temple visit of the New Year, so…"

Kojou, gazing at the fruitless antagonism burning between Asagi and Yume, shook his head in resignation. Then a different voice called:

"Aiba, have some water. Yume, you, too."

"Miss Yukina…?"

"She came out of Kojou's kitchen like it was nothing, didn't she…?"

Yume's and Asagi's cheeks twitched as they noticed Yukina coming in carrying glasses of ice water.

Wearing street clothes and an apron, Yukina blended naturally with the Akatsuki residence's scenery, giving off the impression that this was where she belonged. Seeing Yukina like that caused the spirit of competition to burn even brighter within Asagi and Yume.

"Er, no, with Nagisa gone for homecoming, I thought I'd help prepare for New Year's in her stead…"

Yukina hastily excused herself, but this only heightened Asagi's and Yume's sense of defeat. The two had gone to extraneous lengths to get dolled up in a roundabout attempt to win Kojou over, yet Yukina had infiltrated and occupied Kojou's kitchen ahead of them. Naturally, they were seething over their strategic error.

Yaze, gazing at all this from afar, realized that the room smelled of Yukina's shampoo and made a leering, amused smile as he said:

"Oooh… Yukina, you're pretty sexy when you're just out of the bath."

"Eh? I-is that so…?"

The joking way Yaze made the assertion threw Yukina off a little. Yaze touched his hand to his chin, nodding like a detective in a rocking chair just after making a clever deduction.

"Wait a minute… Nagisa's gone, so that means Kojou and Yukina have been here all this time by themselves. For some reason, the two were worn out, had already bathed, and on top of that, the bedroom door, which is usually closed, is open for some reason… Ah!"

"'Ah,' my ass! It's just spring cleaning, or rather, my mom ransacked the whole place, and cleaning *that* up is why we're exhausted—that's all!"

"What are you saying in front of an elementary schooler, idiot?!"

Yaze let out an anguished groan as Kojou and Asagi slapped him from both sides.

"That hurt. Geez, all I said was *Ah*!"

"Oh, shut up."

Ignoring Yaze's objection and his painful groan, Kojou, thoroughly exhausted, turned to the kid. "More to the point, why is Yume with you anyway?"

"Ah…well, that's because my big bro is li'l Yume's guardian on paper, y'see. So since Tensou Academy's elementary school dormitory is closed for New Year's Eve, the Yaze family's takin' care of her. Then li'l Yume said she reaaaally wanted to see you, so I went all out of my way to—"

Yaze, trying to explain even though no one had asked him to, shouted "Ow!" and pressed a hand to the bridge of his nose as he reeled backward. Yume had used the sleeve of her kimono like a whip to smack Yaze in the face.

"Please do not speak of things that do not concern you. Also, I believe I have asked you not to use that weird nickname."

"Ugh…"

That little brat, Yaze thought as he glared at Yume, his lips pursed in frustration. "Hmph," Yume fumed, turning her face aside, spurning Yaze. Ever since their first meeting, they just hadn't gotten along very well.

During all that time, the water came to a boil. On Itogami Island, land of eternal summer, New Year's soba was still normal soba noodles. During the time Yukina was boiling the noodles, Kojou was preparing green onions and other condiments.

"Kinda late to notice this, but since I've been on this island, New Year's Eve never really feels like a celebration."

Kojou listened to the voices of crickets outside the window as he unwittingly let his true feelings slip. As a Demon Sanctuary, Itogami Island inevitably had a large overseas-born population, and thanks to the climate, there was little to separate the seasons. He'd seen the excitement on a music TV channel on public broadcasting, but it felt like something happening in a far-off nation.

"I suppose so. Motoki and I have lived here since we were kids, so we're used to it, I guess."

"Thank you for the meal," said Asagi before having some of her noodles.

"We might be doin' the first temple visit, but the countdown to New Year's fireworks is the main event," Yaze said. "It's a pain in the neck, so I'll just loaf around at Kojou's place. It'll be about time to tuck li'l Yume into bed by then, too." Lying slovenly on the sofa, he gave Yume's head a little pat.

She brusquely brushed Yaze's hand aside and insisted, "Please do not treat me like a child. I have no trouble with staying up late. I'm a succubus, after all. You could even say that I'm currently in my element."

"You just want to see the fireworks."

"I—I do not!"

When Yaze made this assertion, Yume's face went scarlet as she shook her head.

However, behind her strong statement, she seemed sleepy even then, perhaps physically worn out from wearing the long-sleeved kimono. She was blinking more frequently, and she'd barely touched the candy.

"It sure would be nice for it to cool down a bit so we could go out in these outfits, though..."

Asagi seemed to be speaking to herself—and not out of any consideration for Yume—as she let her real thoughts slip. *Where'd that 'pride as a woman' run off to?* thought Kojou, smiling a bit.

"Well, having you endure it and collapse won't do anyone any good. How 'bout changing clothes?" he asked.

"S...sure..."

Asagi appeared conflicted as she put a hand on the cord and belt keeping her waist taut. To Asagi, a glutton in spite of her appearance, the fact that she couldn't eat a meal as she pleased while wearing a long-sleeved outfit was an unexpected miscalculation. The issue of whether she'd already succeeded in her objective of showing off to Kojou in her outfit seemed to weigh heavily on her mind.

"Um...if you are going to change clothes, how about I take a picture first?"

As Yukina spoke, she brought out the digital camera she'd just gotten from Mimori. Apparently, she thought she should photograph Asagi and Yume after they had put so much effort into their appearances.

Asagi, her interest piqued, went "Wow!" as her eyes sparkled. "That's an MAR Zeta 9, isn't it? You bought it?"

"No, it was a gift. Mimori said it was in lieu of a New Year's present…"

"You're kidding me. I'm a little jealous. That model isn't even on sale in Japan…!"

Asagi's brows furled as she gnawed her chopsticks in envy. Asagi, a computer nut, had a soft spot for rare digital devices.

"Er, in other words, that camera's pretty good stuff?"

For his part, Kojou had little interest in such gadgets; if anything, he was more interested in how Asagi ate.

Asagi nodded strongly. "Yeah, very much so. It's water-resistant and impact-resistant—the sensor's HQ is connected to the Net, and the imaging system specs are pretty high up, too…but the real selling point is definitely the new model of DSP. These have proprietary MAC units… They say processing efficiency is increased by two orders of magnitude."

"R-right…"

I get that I don't get it at all, thought Kojou, nodding weakly.

During that time, Asagi continued to gaze covetously at Yukina's camera when she said, "Right. After you take the photo, how about you send it to me later?"

"Ah, yes. If you teach me how, then certainly…"

Yukina nodded a half-hearted *yes*. Yukina had a great deal of knowledge about anything related to rituals, but when it came to operating machinery, she was all thumbs.

"Ah, right… We'd have to pair it. Himeragi, do you have a PC?"

"No." Yukina shook her head. "I'm sorry."

"Hmm." Asagi's shoulders dipped in dismay. Normally, the Cyber Empress walked around with multiple devices—notebook PC, tablet, etc.—but unsurprisingly, that was not the case while she walked around in a kimono.

"Kojou, don't you have one?"

"Ah… There's the one Nagisa uses once in a while."

Kojou opened a cabinet standing in a corner of the living room. Inside was a hand-me-down laptop from Mimori. For people living on Itogami Island, whether it was clothing, pets, or sports gear, if you wanted anything even a little exotic, you had to get it online. That was how Kojou and Nagisa came to acquire bare-minimum computing skills.

"Can I borrow it?"

"Sure thing. It's not like it's Nagisa's alone."

"I'll help myself, then."

With his permission, Asagi opened the laptop. Then, the instant she turned on the power...

"Uwaa..."

Asagi murmured as she knelt on the spot. Stickers with what were apparently Nagisa's username and log-in password were stuck on the top of the computer keyboard. To Asagi, an expert in cracking passwords, the level of security was so wide open that she must have wondered if someone was playing tricks on her.

"Simply logging in like this is kind of a blow to my pride as a hacker, but..."

Grimacing at the indignity, Asagi connected Yukina's camera to the laptop. For all its high specs, the MAR digital camera had numerous install options that needed to be set, and inputting all that was a chore. Using a laptop greatly reduced the time and trouble involved.

"Well, fine. For now, I'll just do the camera settings, select Himeragi's photo, and send it to my address... Hmm?"

Asagi was tapping away at the settings when her hand came to a stop, like she'd just noticed something.

"What is it?"

Kojou peered over Asagi's shoulder. *I don't like this*, her bitten lip seemed to suggest.

"This account... It looks like it's synchronized with Nagisa's smartphone account..."

"Synchronized?"

"It's set so data is exchanged between the smartphone and the computer. It's convenient because you can check the e-mail inbox and appointments put into the calendar and so on from both ends."

"Ahh, that I get, but..."

In other words, she was apparently able to browse part of the data on Nagisa's smartphone. The feature may have been convenient, but in terms of privacy, it was dangerous, too.

"Is there some kind of bad data in there...?"

"Not the kind of bad you're imagining."

When Kojou leaned forward, anxious about e-mails from boys or similar things, Asagi sullenly brushed him aside. Then Asagi opened an image file.

"See, Nagisa took this photo from her smartphone. The data's corrupted, so it's only displaying about half of it…"

"…Huh?" Kojou furled his brows, unable to grasp the image's significance. "What the hell?"

The photo's date and time were from about a week prior—the day Nagisa arrived at Tangiwa, her grandmother's hometown. It was also the day after all contact with her had been cut.

The lower half of the image had damaged data, taking on a mosaic pattern. And the upper half of the image was the night sky.

The image was probably taken through a car window. A mountain ridge cut through the winter sky. The moon and stars were not visible above it. Darkness spread across the screen as if it was the deep ocean floor.

And an odd pattern was floating within that darkness.

There were concentric circles, layer upon layer. Sorcerous runes were inscribed on their inner edges.

The giant pattern of glimmering light covered the whole nighttime sky…

…like a net, trapping Nagisa and others within.

"That's—?!"

"A magic circle…?!"

Kojou and Yukina met each other's faces as their breath caught in their throats.

It was the night of December 31—the Demon Sanctuary of Itogami Island, far removed from the mainland.

One hour and fifty minutes remained until the New Year…

CHAPTER TWO
SHADOWS
OF INTRIGUE

1

The New Year's Eve bells began to ring.

It was just past eleven fifteen PM. The announcer's voice over the radio was rambling about the state of the entire country of Japan just before the New Year.

Motoki Yaze, sitting in the back seat of a taxi, grimaced as the noise filled the air while he pressed a cell phone to his ear. The other person on the line was Kazuma Yaze, his half brother who was ten years his senior.

After spending thirty seconds on hold, Yaze was starting to get irritated, but then he finally heard his brother get on the line.

"—It's me, Big Bro."

"I know. Motoki, what of Yume?"

The first thing Kazuma had asked about was Yume, making no effort to hide his displeasure. That fact elicited a small, strained smile from Yaze.

Even if it was just on paper, Kazuma was Yume's guardian, and the power she possessed—that of Lilith, the Witch of the Night—made her a precious pawn of the Gigafloat Management Corporation. Even if Kazuma's concern was based on such calculations, Yaze still found it oddly amusing that his calm, rational half brother was giving an elementary school girl such special attention.

"Li'l Yume is sleeping. I'm bringing her home with me right now."

Yaze glanced at the little girl sleeping right beside him as he made his report. Maybe it was exhaustion from being unaccustomed to her outfit, but Yume was sound asleep by the time eleven PM rolled around. Left with no other option, Yaze was in the process of taking her to his home. "More importantly, something kinda troublesome popped up. I want info."

"Sorry, but I'm already past my regular bedtime. If you need something, talk to me tomorrow," Kazuma gently rebuffed.

"Bedtime? It's New Year's Eve."

"Dates are mere symbols humans employ for their own convenience. I have no reason to obey such strictures."

"You will *never* land a woman."

Yaze responded to his half brother's cold reaction with harsh cynicism. He knew the busy Kazuma was very fussy about time, but not even listening to what his younger brother had to say was taking it too far. Yaze couldn't live with himself if he didn't get in at least one invective word.

However, Kazuma didn't pay him the slightest bit of concern as he said, *"If you have a monitoring report, tell it to the Information Department. Hanegiwa should still be there."*

"I'm talking to you because I don't think it's something Ryoko can handle."

"...Explain. Make it brief."

Perhaps Yaze's desperate persistence had conveyed his haste, for Kazuma grudgingly opened the conversation. However, because he'd said *Make it brief,* Yaze's response was not long-winded.

"Nagisa might've been caught up in some kind of incident."

"Nagisa Akatsuki...the Fourth Primogenitor's younger sister. I heard she had gone off the island, yes?"

"Tell me her current circumstances. You're monitoring her, aren't you?"

Yaze wasted no time in issuing his demand. Even if her possession by Root Avrora was temporary, it didn't change that the girl known as Nagisa Akatsuki was such an important individual that even the Gigafloat Management Corporation was concerned. He hardly needed to ask if she was allowed to leave the island without being monitored; it was unthinkable by nature.

That was why Kazuma's reply was tinged with an unmistakable bitterness.

"We lost her. It was right after she arrived on the mainland."

"They shook off the tail?"

"They apparently used an amusement park crowd."

The displeasure in Kazuma's tone increased. For the methodical Kazuma, a subordinate's failure throwing his plans awry was humiliation difficult to endure.

"The handiwork of Kojou's dad, huh…?"

"Most likely. Gajou Akatsuki, the Death Returnee, would appear to be an even more troublesome opponent than rumored."

The old man really got us, thought a flabbergasted Yaze. At minimum, the observer dispatched by the Gigafloat Management Corporation had to be a Hyper Adapter like Yaze—not an opponent that a middle-aged man who wasn't even an Attack Mage could handle under normal circumstances.

"So in the end, we don't know what kind of trouble Nagisa's gotten caught up in… That's not good."

"Why have you deemed her situation perilous?"

Yaze's face twisted in unease as Kazuma calmly posed the question.

"All contact with Nagisa cut off a week ago. But apparently, this was a photo left behind from her smartphone. Can you see it?"

"A magic circle… A rather large-scale one at that," Kazuma murmured after checking the file his brother sent him. *"Certainly, using this level of spell in a Demon Sanctuary is out of the ordinary, to say nothing of magic use on the mainland. However, you cannot judge that Nagisa Akatsuki has become involved in an incident based on this information alone."*

"I see what you're gettin' at. The Corporation can't flex its muscles off the island, right?"

"Correct, particularly when this image is the only confirmation that something occurred."

Kazuma's tone was blunt and dismissive as usual. However, Yaze fully expected as much.

Itogami Island was considered part of Tokyo Metropolis, but the Demon Sanctuary was close to a de facto autonomous territory. If the Gigafloat Management Corporation ventured beyond the Demon Sanctuary, its various rights were rescinded. The organization was not permitted to dispatch the Island Guard's law enforcement units off the island, even to rescue a civilian.

If push came to shove, however, that logic was nothing more than a front.

"And if I told you that Kojou is making noise about it?"

Yaze played his card strategically. Politics had a facade, a back side, and a gray area between the two sides. Demon Sanctuaries existed to govern that third, uncertain realm—and the people that lived within it.

If you had a card that trumped that false front—some kind of fake justification—you could make your move.

"He's got a pretty serious sister complex, you know. If we don't play this right, I can't say he won't rush right out of Itogami Island and look for Nagisa himself."

"The Fourth Primogenitor having a sister complex is news to me."

Kazuma's voice did not waver. He'd no doubt expected Yaze to play that card.

"Well, fine. I understand the situation. I will add more investigators to search for more information. At this stage, it is unwise to dispatch Attack Mages in excess, however, we cannot simply let the situation lie."

"I suppose realistically that's all we can do."

Yaze exhaled, dispirited. Even if she was related to the Fourth Primogenitor, Nagisa Akatsuki was an ordinary person, not a demon. Dispatching investigators at all was the largest concession Kazuma could make. For now, Yaze was forced to accept that.

"Roger. What do we do with Kojou, then?"

The mood was heavy. Yaze was not confident they could keep the World's Mightiest Vampire under control when he was half crazed from obscure information suggesting his little sister might be in trouble.

However, Kazuma's reply was unexpectedly brief.

"Continue monitoring him. If necessary, we will deal with him."

"Deal with him... Big Bro, you can't mean...?"

"Do not make me repeat myself. Continue monitoring him."

Kazuma gruffly hung up on him. Yaze slumped his shoulders into the seat of the taxi. Beside him, Yume, in her long-sleeved kimono, was deeply, innocently asleep.

The change of date would soon be at hand...

2

A large crowd gazed in awe at the colorful streaks of light filling the night sky.

Boom! The loud bursts resonated across the island. It was the fireworks show for the New Year's countdown.

Kojou and the others looked up at the wild dance of scattering lights in the night sky from the path leading to the temple.

Yukina's eyes were open especially wide as she watched the fireworks. Asagi completely devoted herself to videotaping the fireworks using the digital camera she'd borrowed from Yukina. Kojou, on the other hand, sank his teeth deep into his lower lip, glaring at his cell phone with the look of a man fallen on hard times. With no calls getting through to Nagisa, all he could do was send text after text and pray for a response.

"Calm down, Kojou. We don't know for sure that something's happened to Nagisa."

Asagi, seeing Kojou in a state of mental anguish, spoke like she was at her wit's end. Kojou's shoulders quivered, almost like a child scolded by a pet owner for playing pranks on the poor animal.

"I know that. I'm completely calm."

"This is calm…?"

When Kojou looked back, making excuses with a quivering voice, Asagi sighed. As before, Asagi was in her long-sleeved kimono, but thanks to the temperature having dropped in the middle of the night, she was a bit sprightlier than before.

Incidentally, Kojou was wearing a casual outfit: shorts with a parka on top. Yukina, carrying her guitar case like usual, was wearing bordered knee socks and a miniskirt; she looked like she belonged in an all-girl band.

Meanwhile, the procession of visitors moved in an orderly fashion, and Kojou and the others arrived at the temple's gate.

Itogami Temple, where Kojou and the rest had gone for their first temple visit of the New Year, was a popular spot for such occasions for a simple reason: It was a great place from which to see the fireworks. There were numerous islanders frolicking within the grounds, with numerous night stalls lined up to greet them.

Even amid that jovial atmosphere, Kojou's face refused to crack a smile. With Nagisa unable to take calls, her smartphone had taken a single photo. Its very existence robbed Kojou of the ability to calm down. His gloomy attitude definitely put a damper on the general mood of the highly anticipated New Year's temple visit, but because Asagi and Yukina knew why he was feeling down, they were in no position to complain.

"Well, why don't we pray? This temple is supposed to be blessed by a god, you know."

Perhaps Asagi tossed up such irresponsible words because she couldn't think of any better way to cheer Kojou up. With eyes like a dead fish, he sluggishly gazed at the sign standing before the temple.

"According to this, the god of this temple presides over prosperity in wealth and marriage...," he said.

"Hey, it's a god. It can fulfill a request or two outside of its specialties, right?"

Whether her argument was convincing or not, Asagi firmly presented the uncertain logic.

"Come to think of it, senpai, how did your fortune drawing go?"

Yukina rather forcefully changed the subject, perhaps hoping to brush the negative atmosphere aside.

Itogami Temple's sacred lots were not mere tests of chance; rather, they were exceptionally accurate oracles produced with Demon Sanctuary technology. Considering Kojou's current troubles, the odds were high that he had obtained beneficial advice from his drawings.

"...Senpai?"

However, Kojou remained silent as he offered Yukina his two sacred lots. Taking them, Yukina was aghast—for the two lots Kojou had drawn were stamped with the characters for *bad* and *very bad*, respectively. Apparently, Kojou had been unnerved after having initially drawn *bad*, redrawing only to get *very bad* instead.

"Umm...it is all right, senpai. If right now is rock bottom, it should only get better from here."

"Right, right. Your misfortune might mean Nagisa has good fortune dancing all around her."

"Yeah...well, not that it really matters to me right now— Ow!"

Kojou, largely the author of his own worries, spoke in a listless tone.

Then, he suddenly felt a dull pain from the back of his head. Coins that someone had tossed toward the offering box had struck his head instead.

"Wh-what the hell?!"

As he continued to stand there, Kojou was grazed by other coins tossed toward the offering box. It was a common sight at a temple with so many visitors, but Kojou felt like a lot more coins were landing direct hits that year. He feared this was the result of his *very bad* fortune.

Yukina drew close to Kojou's ear, whispering in a small voice, "Senpai, perhaps someone is aiming at you? Somehow, I am sensing some kind of ill will toward you…"

At that moment, the number of coins pouring down on him noticeably increased. Someone definitely had it out for him.

"Kojou, maybe someone's jealous of you? You have Himeragi with you, after all."

"No, Aiba, I believe you stand out far more in that kimono than I do right now…"

"Well, a lot of guys come to pray at a temple of marriage because they want girlfriends. He's walking with a beauty on either side of him, so of course they'll send hate his way."

"What kind of logic is that?! And it's not like we're 'together' like that to begin with…!"

Venting to no one in particular, Kojou prayed in a hurry and fled the space in front of the offering box. Yukina and Asagi paid him no heed, remaining in place as they each offered prayers before the hall of worship.

Perhaps they prayed for the safety of Nagisa, their friend. Perhaps they asked for something else. Either way, it was not for Kojou to know.

Even then, the sound of fireworks celebrating the New Year continued to echo.

As he waited for Asagi and Yukina to finish their temple visit, Kojou pulled out his cell phone and stared at it again. The LCD screen displayed that night-sky photo, sent to him from the laptop.

When Asagi and Yukina met up with him after praying, he asked the following question just in case: "This image… There's no way this is just fireworks, right?"

Giant patterns filled the night sky above them. Artificial radiance danced in the heavens. In that regard, the two scenes did have something

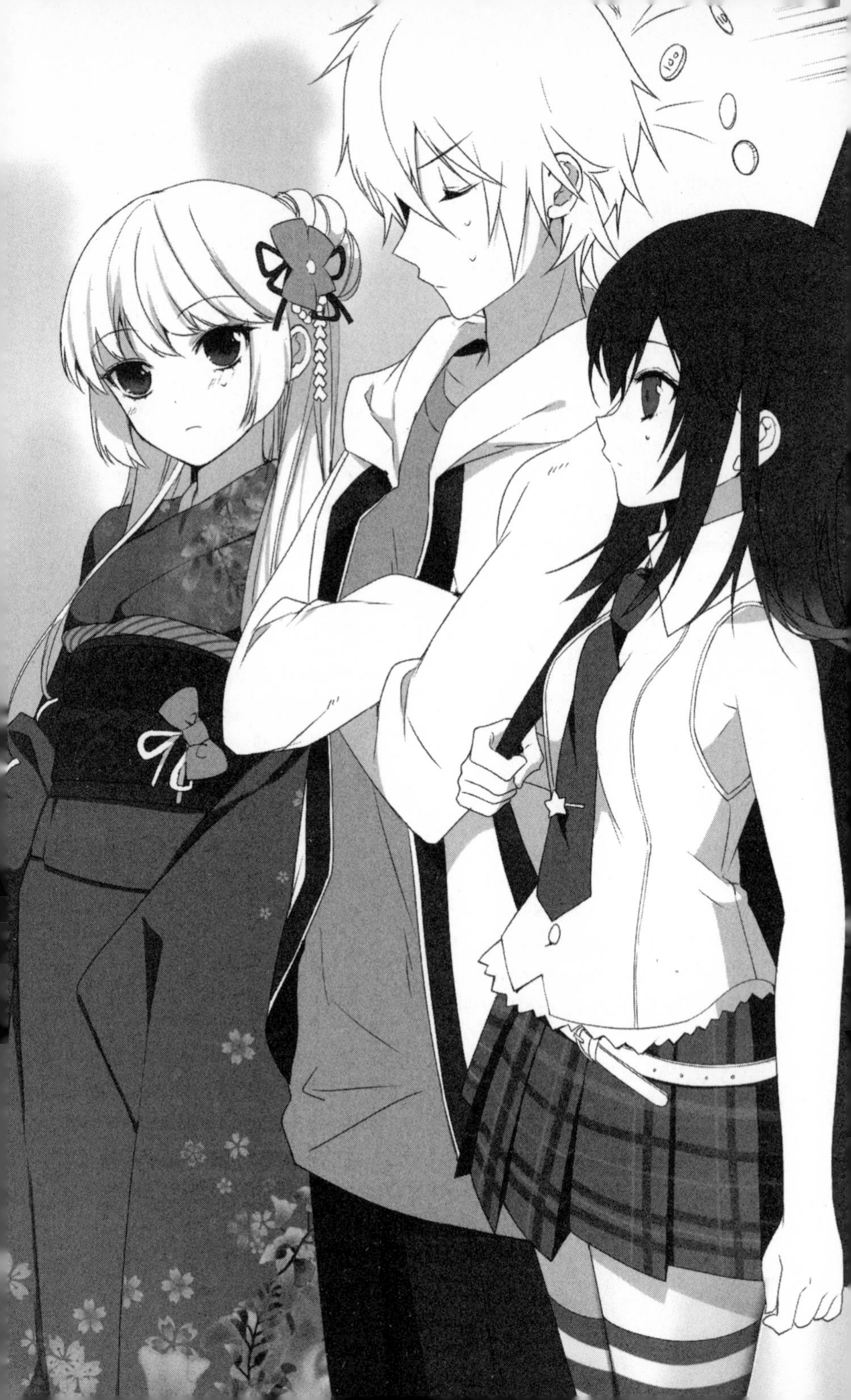

in common. But without any hesitation, the two girls ruled out the possibility.

"I don't think there's any way. Besides, digital data can be falsified in all kinds of ways. There's no need to brood over it this much, I think."

"I suppose not. Even if it was a magic circle, it does not mean it was targeting Nagisa specifically."

"But there's no proof it wasn't, right?"

Kojou clutched his head, envisioning the worst-case scenario. Asagi might have felt annoyed at that point, for she ignored Kojou and turned toward Yukina.

"Come to think of it, don't you know what this is? What magic circle it is—with what effects?"

"I am sorry. I do not know that much...though Sayaka might know what it is..."

"Kirasaka...?"

Kojou, hearing Yukina's explanation, lifted his face with a start.

Like Yukina, Sayaka Kirasaka was an Attack Mage belonging to the Lion King Agency. She had been granted the title of Shamanic War Dancer, an expert in curses and assassination.

"Actually, this magic circle kinda looks like..."

"Sayaka's Lustrous Scale, yes?"

Yukina nodded in response to Kojou's murmur. She'd probably noticed that from the very beginning.

The pattern of light captured by Nagisa's photograph greatly resembled a large-scale magic circle created by one of Sayaka Kirasaka's whistling arrows. The pattern's shape and fine details differed, but its size, and the fact it was written into the sky above, were identical.

"Does someone else have a bow and arrows like Sayaka...?"

"No. Der Freischötz is difficult to handle, and I have heard that Sayaka is the only one who can properly employ it. The ritual energy required to activate it is off the scale, and the compatibility requirements are exceptionally severe."

"Oh...? That's kinda surprising, somehow."

This was the Lustrous Scale that Sayaka had used to try to slice him in half and blast him to death in a jealous rage, waving it around however she pleased, but it was, appearances aside, a surprisingly delicate weapon.

"But there were rumors a while back that they had generated a mass-production model with simplified construction based on Lustrous Scale data…"

"A mass-production model?"

"Yes."

"So using that, other casters could use the same spells Kirasaka does…?"

"I believe so. However, that should not be…"

Yukina faintly lowered her eyes as she hesitated in her words.

Using a mass-produced Der Freischötz, it was possible that someone other than Sayaka had traced a magic circle in the sky. However, that did not change the fact that the mass-production model was a Lion King Agency construct.

In other words, it was indeed someone related to the Lion King Agency who had involved Nagisa in an incident.

"Shit," Kojou spat as he checked his cell phone's incoming call history. He picked out a suitable number and called it.

"Senpai?"

"I'll try asking Sayaka. If this really was the Lion King Agency's doing, she might know something about it."

Off to the side, Asagi glared at Kojou, displeasure plain on her face.

"Why do you know Kirasaka's phone number?"

"I'm not really sure why, but I talk to her over the phone every once in a while. She calls sometimes."

"You *what*?!"

"I said I'm not really sure why."

At first, Sayaka called with openers such as *Tell me how Yukina's been doing*, but lately, her topics for conversation often strayed outside that: grumbling about her superiors or asking his opinion on new snacks—subjects Kojou cared little about. Since it wasn't hurting anyone, Kojou didn't mind.

"What's wrong?"

"I'm not getting through. Or rather, it says this number is no longer in use."

And at a time like this, thought Kojou, glaring at the phone in irritation.

The corners of Asagi's lips curled up in delight as she teased, "Couldn't it be that she's simply blocking your calls? Oh, Kojou, what did you do?"

"What, it's my fault?!"

"In other words, you've had a falling out with Sayaka? Why...?"

"Did you ask her something rude? Like her bust size, or her bra size, or perhaps her *three sizes?*"

"Like hell I would! What use would there be askin' stuff like that?!"

Asagi ignored Kojou's pleas of innocence and exhaled.

Though her words were blunt, they really nagged at Kojou somehow. The coincidences fit together, and the timing made sense.

Losing contact with Nagisa and their father. Sayaka blocking his calls. Neither were particularly big things in and of themselves. However, lined up one after another, these facts painted a picture that wasn't pretty. He felt like his vision was being obstructed by an invisible wall of malicious intent.

"Himeragi, can't you contact the Lion King Agency?"

"Of course, I can send an inquiry, but with only Nagisa's photo to go on, I'm not sure how much I'll be able to ask of anyone..."

"That's more of a pain than I thought it'd be."

"It is..."

Yukina bit her lip and nodded. Kojou remained silent and closed the unresponsive flip phone.

Asagi gazed at the two of them and shrugged her shoulders, almost like she was getting something off her back.

"Well, if that's how it is, there's no way around it," she said.

"What are you talking about?"

Sensing the suspicion in Kojou's question, Asagi coughed ever so slightly. The peculiar air of tension she radiated made Kojou's expression harden in turn.

"W-well, you see, Kojou... Tonight, both my parents are out, and no one's around, so..."

Asagi drew in her breath and steeled her resolve, her cheeks reddening. She squirmed slightly, entwined her two index fingers, and with upturned eyes, she shifted her gaze toward Kojou and continued, "Wanna come to my place?"

Faced with Asagi's abrupt invitation, Kojou didn't move a muscle, cell phone still in hand.

As Kojou and Asagi locked eyes, Yukina could only stare at them, astonished.

3

The Aiba residence was on the eastern beach of Island West. Rare for Itogami Island, the houses were separate and lined up in a row on prime real estate surrounded by lush trees.

"…Come to think of it, this is the first time I've been to Asagi's place," Kojou murmured, deeply impressed as he observed the oriental-style mansion.

According to Asagi, this was the first time she'd invited a friend over to her place. It seemed the odd tension in Asagi's voice when she'd invited him was nothing more than that.

"It is an incredible house…"

Yukina also voiced her admiration as she looked up at the enormous metal gate.

On Itogami Island, a man-made isle with astronomical land prices compared to the mainland, a separate house was a considerable extravagance by itself. Even among the others at the site, the Asagi residence stood out from the pack with its sheer size; the mansion had clearly been built with a lot of money invested into it.

"We have to live here because it's convenient for security purposes. It's an old building, so don't get your hopes up about the inside," Asagi said nonchalantly as she disarmed the security at the entrance.

Kojou knew she wasn't being modest—she was speaking the truth.

This was the Demon Sanctuary of Itogami Island. There was no way Asagi would live on an island like that if she were simply another rich man's daughter. She had domestic circumstances of her own.

"Wait here while I clean up the room. It'll only take five minutes," she said firmly, leading Kojou and Yukina past the entrance, which was nicely air-conditioned. There was even a bench for guests.

Even though the wait wasn't an issue for Kojou, he asked, "Want a hand with the cleaning?"

"Just wait here!"

He was only trying to be considerate, but Asagi's eyebrows rose as she glared at him. *Peek and I'll kill you,* her look suggested. Apparently, she was ditching Kojou because there was something she really didn't want him to see.

After Asagi left, Yukina gazed at the entrance and quietly murmured, "Security certainly is tight here."

Kojou seemed a little surprised as he looked around the area. "You can tell?"

"I do not know about the mechanical trappings, but it uses a fairly high-end enchantment for repelling intruders, and a curse reflection ward besides."

"Huh." Kojou nodded in admiration.

"Well that's 'cause Asagi's dad is an Itogami City councilor."

"Councilor?"

"It's kind of like a city parliament. Apparently, that's how Asagi was brought to the island."

"Oh..."

Suddenly, Yukina seemed to understand her situation. Many of the students living in the Demon Sanctuary had their own circumstances, and Asagi was no exception to the rule.

She'd been living on Itogami Island since before entering elementary school. At the time, Itogami Island still had numerous law enforcement issues, and many mainlanders looked upon its residents as bizarre. The daughter of a statesman of that same Demon Sanctuary, Asagi couldn't have had an easy time growing up. That she never talked about it was probably her pride at work.

"Oh my... Guests?"

Perhaps Kojou and Yukina's conversation had been overheard. They noticed the patter of someone rushing down a corridor, and an unfamiliar woman poked her head in. She had an unadorned and fairly youthful look. Her long, tied-up black hair went nicely with her light velvet kimono.

As Kojou and Yukina stood rooted at the entrance, she gave them a smile of approval, almost like an innocent child's.

"Sorry for imposing."

Kojou and Yukina reflexively bowed their heads before they could think of anything else. *I thought no one was supposed to be here*, he grumbled at Asagi in his own mind.

"H-happy New Year."

"Happy New Year."

Seeing Yukina's awkward greeting, the woman's eyes narrowed in delight. It was a shockingly friendly attitude toward visitors arriving in the dead of the first night of the New Year.

"Friends of Asagi, yes? Splendid. To think she would bring friends here. You must be hot over there. Come on in—no need to be so reserved."

"Um, uhh… Asagi…said to stay right here, so—"

"By any chance, would you be Kojou?"

Just as Kojou was trying to beat a hasty retreat, he was intercepted by the woman's direct line of questioning.

"Yes. Kojou Akatsuki."

"My, is that so…? So you're the one. Tee-hee—I'm glad to finally meet you… And this lovely young lady must be Himeragi. Nagisa is off to see family, yes?"

"Y-yes. Pleased to meet you."

Yukina, completely swept up in the kimono-clad woman's momentum, bowed her head once more. The woman's inquisitive eyes glimmered as they scrutinized the pair's reactions. Though her demeanor was pleasant, it was oddly difficult to get in a word with her. They were going on the assumption that she was Asagi's mother, so they didn't know how to react.

"Aaah…?!"

Asagi, returning from tidying up her room, noticed the woman's presence and let out a puzzled yelp.

"Sumire, what are you doing here?! Weren't you supposed to be going back to your parents' place tonight?!"

"Sensai's work ran late, so the schedule changed."

As she gave her reply with the utmost nonchalance, Sumire Aiba lifted her head to see Asagi standing on the ascending stairway.

Sumire was Asagi's father's second wife; in other words, Asagi's stepmother. It seemed like the relationship between Asagi and Sumire was a bit complicated—not exactly bad, but it looked like Asagi had a hard time dealing with her stepmother, though that didn't seem to be the case the other way around.

"After such a long trip, you simply must relax for a while. I'll prepare some tea. We even have the Iris House *dorayaki* Asagi is so fond of. Those little red-bean pancakes really are quite tasty."

"Never mind that. No need for snacks today. I just brought them here 'cause there's something I need to take care of in a hurry."

Asagi was desperately trying to shoo her stepmother away. However, Sumire displayed the mysterious strength of her persistence as she said, "Is that so? But they've come all this way..."

"You two go ahead without me! Up the stairs—it's the room on the right!"

"Ah...pardon us. Let's go, Himeragi."

"Right."

Thus ordered by Asagi, who sounded like she had her back against the wall, Kojou and Yukina ascended the stairs which were made from a rare breed of tree native to Itogami Island, something flat-out extravagant.

Upon locating the room Asabi mentioned, Kojou opened the door and went inside.

Boasting a baby-blue and pink color scheme, it was a stereotypical girl's room.

A closet was crammed chock-full of Western-style clothing. Various magazines, cosmetics, and stuffed animals were strewn around the room. There was a school uniform on a hangar on the wall, perhaps fresh from dry cleaning. The scattered pillows and rumpled sheets made the room appear very lived-in. Of course, Kojou, whose little sister would be furious if he was ever caught in her room without permission, could not help feeling a bit unnerved.

"So this is Asagi's room... Well, it suits her."

"Is it really all right for us to let ourselves in?" Yukina asked without budging.

"She told us to, so it should be fine," Kojou answered, almost for his own benefit.

It being an unfamiliar room of a female classmate made it hard to relax, but on the other hand, devices characteristic of Asagi's other side were there as well: a Spartan, office-use monitor and a rack-style PC cluster. She did most of her part-time job from home, so she had a ridiculously high-spec computer. The instant he noticed its presence, Kojou faintly understood just why Asagi had invited them to her room in the first place.

"Sorry for the wait. Sit wherever you'd like."

Asagi returned to the room, carrying a tray packed with tea cakes and drinks. Surely, her looking fairly exhausted wasn't just a figment of Kojou's imagination.

"You didn't go and touch anything you weren't supposed to, did you, Kojou?"

"I did not. More importantly, is everything okay with Sumire? You didn't get much of a chance to say hi…"

"It's fine. To be honest, I didn't even expect to see her tonight."

Asagi spoke through a pout like a stubborn child's.

But after placing the tray on a table, Asagi sat at her computer and revealed an impetuous smile, like she was finally back in her own element.

"More to the point, you want to know how Nagisa's doing at the moment, right? Just wait a sec—I'll check things out."

"'Check things out'? What do you think you're gonna do? I don't think Grandma's temple is connected to the Net," he asserted with a rueful tone.

It was a low-tech, run-down temple to begin with, plus it was in a mountain range where even cell tower signals could not reach. He didn't think Asagi could check on Nagisa's safety against that backdrop no matter how good a hacker she was.

However, as if such things were minor inconveniences, Asagi smiled boldly and said:

"Computers aren't just for checking the inside of buildings. Mogwai, put the data I extracted through these filters."

"My goodness, we only just started the new year. You really run your AI ragged, li'l miss."

An oddly human-sounding synthetic voice could be heard over the speakers of Asagi's computer. This was the avatar of the five supercomputers that controlled Itogami Island—the supporting AI that Asagi had dubbed Mogwai.

"Stop flapping your lips and do it!"

"Yeah, yeah. Happy New Year...aaand—!"

Mogwai began analyzing the image according to the program Asagi had input.

Mogwai had a calculation ability on par with the finest in the world, but it was quirky and difficult to use; it was said that Itogami Island had virtually no engineers able to bring out its full potential. But for some reason, it got along with Asagi and dutifully followed her orders—and hers alone. Thus, in the blink of an eye, Asagi and Mogwai completed complex work that would have taken ordinary engineers months to finish.

The screen displayed a shady-looking man with a trench coat and a lively looking middle school girl walking around an airport: Gajou and Nagisa Akatsuki.

"Surveillance cameras...!" Kojou exclaimed when he realized what he was looking at.

Even as he did, the images of Gajou and Nagisa were continually replaced. Using the security cameras in the airport and matching running the image through Itogami Island's face recognition data, Asagi was analyzing their every movement.

"There are aircraft boarding records, after all, so I thought I'd retrace their path from that point on. If I can get to the credit card history, I'll know what they bought, too."

Asagi proudly thrust out her chest, looking very satisfied with herself. Kojou understood the logic of it, but actually executing it had to be far easier said than done. She was invading the servers of public infrastructure and credit card companies, stealing their data, and isolating it to those two individuals. It was enough to make your head spin.

However, if she kept this up, it was indeed possible to check on Nagisa's current whereabouts.

"Incredible..."

"This is the so-called surveillance society, huh?"

Yukina exhaled in admiration as Kojou's shoulders cringed in fear.

"Keh-keh." Mogwai laughed cynically right around when Gajou and Nagisa were coming out of an airport lobby.

"Daddy got a rental car at the airport—under a false name."

"What's my dumb dad using an alias for…?"

Thanks to Mogwai, nothing came of it, but if circumstances were different, they might have lost track of Gajou and Nagisa then and there. No, clearly that was Gajou's intention. He was acting with all the caution of a mafia boss. *Geez, just how shady are you?* wondered Kojou, beside himself.

Asagi was using police license-plate-recognition cameras to follow Gajou's car along the freeway. It was a system that checked license plate numbers to assist in searching for wanted criminals.

However, Asagi nervously exclaimed, "Huh?! There's no route data left… He switched license plates?! Since when?!"

"Keh-keh… Thorough one, ain't he? I'll find him using driver-image data."

"From Haneda, he headed for Tokyo…but he got off the freeway just before Shibuya."

"Shibuya?" Kojou asked.

Why'd he go to a place like that? he wondered, knitting his brows. It was still a considerable distance to Grandma's place in Tangiwa.

"There's a purchase record from a secondhand clothing store in Harajuku… Also, they stopped for cake and drinks."

"That's a store Nagisa wanted to go to. She said she learned about it from a TV show a while back," Yukina added, albeit reluctantly.

What the heck is she doing? thought Kojou, amazed. Incidentally, at around the same time, he was back on Itogami Island being attacked and nearly killed by Divine Beasts and an evil deity, but that was another story.

"They checked in to a hotel and… What is this, a strip club?"

Asagi checked the ticket from Gajou's credit card purchase history and shot Kojou a look of disgust. Apparently, Gajou had slipped out of the hotel in the dead of night to have some fun at a strip bar.

"I don't know anything about that! That moron just did that on his own!"

"They went to Dreamland the next morning, huh…and they stayed at the hotel on the grounds, too."

"Is there even a point to tracking 'em like this…?" Kojou murmured, disheartened.

He'd expected to find out if Nagisa was safe and sound, but before long, it had become an operation to expose the various stupidities of Gajou Akatsuki's actions. The last image on the amusement park security cameras was of Gajou wearing kitty ears on his head, enjoying himself in a manner disgraceful for a man of his age. As his son, Kojou couldn't help but be ashamed.

"They're on the move."

After that came images of Gajou at a cabaret club and Nagisa visiting old friends of hers from her elementary school days who she hadn't seen in ages, both thoroughly enjoying themselves; and after *that*, they finally seemed to remember just where it was they were going in the first place.

After switching to a new rental car, Gajou and Nagisa left the metro. They had finally reached the fourth day since leaving Itogami Island. Seeing this, Kojou breathed a sigh of relief as he said, "Looks like this time they headed for Grandma's place."

"This matches up with the dates on the texts Nagisa sent...," Yukina asserted calmly.

Using the cameras placed along the freeway as a measuring device, it was easy to follow the rental car. Gajou and Nagisa's four-wheel-drive vehicle did not encounter any particular trouble, finally arriving at Kannawa Lake. Kojou and Nagisa's grandmother lived at an old temple constructed on the edge of that artificial lake, the product of Kamioda Dam.

The time stamp on the image data left by Nagisa's smartphone roughly coincided with when Asagi calculated the rental car would have arrived. The difference was about fifteen minutes at most. In other words, Nagisa had witnessed that giant magic circle moments after arriving at the temple they were heading to.

Or perhaps it was possible that the magic circle was triggered precisely because Nagisa and Gajou had arrived.

If the activation of the magic circle waited until their arrival, it would be no mere coincidence: It meant that either Nagisa or Gajou was the target.

"Mogwai, have you noticed?"

"Yeah, it's odd."

For their part, Asagi and Mogwai lowered their voices, apparently sensing that something was off.

"What is?" Kojou asked.

"The travel was too smooth," Asagi replied. "The roads should be packed this time of year, but the car Nagisa and Gajou were traveling in didn't slow down from traffic congestion at all."

However, Kojou didn't really understand why Asagi was so on guard.

"It's not just a coincidence? Besides, GPS systems tell you the shortcuts nowadays, right?"

"Naaah, because the other roads are like this."

Mogwai displayed a road map of the area. Apparently, red dots indicated congested roads. The massive congestion breaking out on the major thoroughfare made it so crammed that you'd think it was faster to get out and walk.

"In Tangiwa District...only the road to Kannawa Lake is clear. It's more like everyone's subconsciously avoiding the road. Maybe they went onto the other roads, making them even more packed."

"Subconsciously avoiding the road...? Hey, you don't mean...?"

"Someone placed an aversion ward...?!"

Kojou and Yukina gasped when they realized the cause of the deviation in traffic.

Without Gajou and Nagisa knowing, someone had cast a curse to drive everyone except them away from Kannawa Lake. Put another way, the ward invited in Nagisa and Gajou—and only them.

Kojou had assumed everything had begun with the magic circle Nagisa had photographed. But he was wrong. This curse was already active before she approached Kannawa Lake.

There was no longer any room for doubt. Someone was after one of them: Gajou or Nagisa.

"There's a ward on the entire area around Kannawa Lake? You can do that?"

"You can. However, it requires considerable preparation and many casters—"

"So it's not the sort of curse a single person can fling, yeah...?"

Irritated, Kojou gritted his teeth.

An aversion ward was Sorcery 101. At one extreme, you could establish a minimum strength ward just by planting a single Do Not Enter sign on the side of the road. The aversion spells used by Yukina and her kind put ritual energy into small objects, but the basic principles didn't change.

But however simple the principle, the power and effort involved in maintaining a ward increased exponentially the more you expanded the scale. Something on the scale of driving all unrelated human beings from Kannawa Lake's environs was a fairly large-scale undertaking.

"Mogwai."

"Got it."

Asagi didn't even need to spell it out for Mogwai to look into it. Once you knew a large organization was in play, deducing its identity was not so difficult. After all, the organizations able to muster an aversion ward of this magnitude were few and far between. Furthermore, the more people involved in something, the more difficult it was to cover it up.

Food, sleep, travel, communications—the traces of the various actions required to sustain activity as a group and the resulting flow of money told you the organization's identity.

"I see. I get how they're doing it."

Mogwai laughed sardonically as he brought up an image on the monitor. It displayed a group of people, all in camouflage and bearing firearms.

"There are reports all around Kannawa Lake that roads are closed due to avalanches or landslides. The Self-Defense Forces have been dispatched in the name of disaster relief."

"Self-Defense Forces...?"

Rather than be surprised, Kojou was simply confused. Certainly, Gajou's semi-criminal fieldwork made him an archeologist of some notoriety, but he wasn't a dangerous enough individual to be targeted by the SDF. That went double for Nagisa, a simple middle schooler. *There has to be some mistake*, he thought.

"But the group actually calling the shots seems to be called the Sorcerous Disaster Commission. They're the ones who put up a spell ward."

"Sorcerous Disaster Commission...?!"

Yukina reacted immediately. Her lips were trembling, and she seemed to be going pale before Kojou's eyes. With a look of shock plain on her face, she trembled as if seized by fear.

"Himeragi?"

"The SDC is one of the Lion King Agency's dummy organizations. Its chief missions are researching ways to avert sorcerous disasters and conveying information to government agencies."

"The Lion King Agency...?! What the heck's going on here...?"

As Yukina explained, her voice sounded faint enough that it seemed it might vanish. Kojou turned a reproachful look toward her.

The Lion King Agency was an organization that defended against large-scale sorcerous disasters and sorcerous terrorism; at the very least, that was what Yukina had told Kojou. Hence, even when he had seen that magic circle, some part of his heart had been at ease. *There's no way the Lion King Agency is after Nagisa*, he thought deep down.

However, the evidence left behind flew in the face of that.

With Yukina at a loss for words, Asagi calmly replied in her place.

"So the SDF and the Lion King Agency are collaborating to seal off Kannawa Lake...in the name of preventing damage from a sorcerous disaster. In other words, this is the reason all contact with Nagisa has been cut off."

"You mean Nagisa's...involved in a sorcerous disaster...?"

"Or maybe they called your li'l sister over to create a sorcerous disaster instead. Keh-keh."

Mogwai's laugh oozed with ill will. The artificial intelligence's words sparked a worry in Kojou he couldn't articulate.

Certainly, Nagisa had been at the center of an enormous sorcerous disaster at one point in the past. That disaster had involved tens of thousands of people, and a gigafloat had sunk as a result. However, that was hardly her fault, and the cause of it was long lost. There was no reason for Nagisa to be related to a sorcerous disaster at that late stage.

Kojou tried to maintain his own calm. Beside him, Yukina's body wobbled heavily.

"The Lion King Agency... No... Why would...?"

Noticing something was wrong, Asagi cried out, "Himeragi...?!"

Yukina, continuing to take shallow breaths, seemed to go dizzy as she collapsed.

"Himeragi?! Hey, Himeragi!"

Held within Kojou's arms, Yukina shook her head, trembling in fear. Then she blacked out completely.

4

The horizon over the water was faintly beginning to brighten as Kojou gazed at it and sighed.

The landscape spread before his eyes was the garden of Asagi's own home. It was not terribly broad, but it was the sort of extravagant, traditional Japanese garden that you never got tired of looking at.

It was almost five in the morning on New Year's Day.

Yukina, who'd had a mild fainting spell, was resting on Asagi's bed.

"I'm gonna get this kimono off now, so scram," said Asagi, driving Kojou out of her room.

He figured mental shock was probably the cause of Yukina's collapse.

Yukina had been shaken by the suspicion that the Lion King Agency had involved Nagisa in an incident—one beyond her expectations. Kojou might be Yukina's target for observation, but Nagisa was different. She was the closest thing to a real friend that Yukina had. Somehow, the Lion King Agency was involved in her disappearance, and without informing Yukina of a single thing—

The shock had apparently hit Yukina, who had been raised by the Lion King Agency from a young age, a lot harder than Kojou thought it would. It wasn't as if she was mentally fragile; if anything, being shaken was the natural reaction. Yukina might have been a Sword Shaman and highly capable in combat, but deep down, she was nothing more than a girl in middle school.

That alone made Kojou unable to blame her in any way.

But on the other hand, he was nervous. For all Kojou knew, Nagisa might be in danger while he was standing there like that. All the same, at that point, Kojou had few cards left to play.

Feeling irritated, like he was slowly being roasted over a high flame, Kojou stood in the garden before the break of dawn. It was then that his feet were assaulted by a sudden impact.

"Aaagh?!"

In danger of losing his balance, Kojou's eyes went wide when he realized what had happened. The first thing his vision caught was a set of sharp canines, followed by eyes with an inquisitive glint.

"A...a dog...?!"

His heart still beating fast from the surprise, Kojou somehow managed to keep the playful pooch at bay. It was a big, muscular dog that seemed over thirty kilograms, and was likely heavily mixed with boxer. Its face was gruff, but it gave off an impression of cheerfulness and intelligence.

Kojou's shock was still raw when he heard a low, calm voice from behind.

"We tried to raise him to be a guard dog, but he's a bit too fond of people."

When Kojou looked back, he saw a casually dressed middle-aged man.

He wasn't all that tall, and his demeanor was, if anything, gentle. However, there was a peculiar air about him. The first word that came to Kojou's mind had three syllables, starting with *ya* and ending in *za*. The man was far more frightening than the scary-faced boxer.

"How is the young lady who came with you?"

The man opened conversation in a gentle tone that belied his appearance.

"I think she's all right by now. Some things happened, and she was caught by surprise a little."

Reflexively, Kojou straightened his back and responded clearly. It was the respectful posture he took toward his elders, which he'd learned in his old athletics club.

"If it is no great matter, that is good, but it is best not to push things too hard… Not for her, and not for you."

The man gave a generous nod as he spoke. That was when Kojou remembered that he already knew who this man was. They had never directly spoken to one another, but he'd seen the man many times. This was Sensai Aiba, Itogami City councilor—Asagi's father.

"Sorry for causing trouble on a day like this."

Kojou apologized to Sensai for imposing in the wee hours of the morning on New Year's Day. However, Sensai shook his head, somehow seeming delighted as he said:

"I don't mind. After all, this is the first time Asagi brought you, her friends, over to visit, and it is not often one has a chance to speak with the World's Mightiest Vampire."

"…?!"

Kojou was unable to keep his face steady in the face of Sensai's casually spoken words. His entire body became slick with sweat as he inquired, largely on reflex:

"You…know about me…?"

"Surely, it is nothing that should surprise you. However I may look, I am an Itogami City councilor. Many people in the Gigafloat Management Corporation are friends of mine. They do try to keep me at least minimally informed about potential dangers that may occur on Itogami Island."

Knowing full well of Kojou's identity, Sensai displayed a composed smile toward him.

"Now that I've broached the subject, may I ask you for one favor?"

"A favor…from me?"

Kojou inquired in a suspicious tone. Even an objective observer would find Sensai's words unexpected.

Certainly, Kojou had obtained the power of the Fourth Primogenitor, but the ability was largely useless beyond indiscriminate destruction. Kojou himself was no more than a poor, powerless student. When it came to living large inside Itogami Island, Sensai had far more power than he did on every front.

Even so, he narrowed his eyes, giving Kojou what somehow seemed like a forlorn look.

"This is probably something only you can do, Akatsuki."

"Huh?"

"The favor is for Asagi. Please make that girl happy."

"……Huh?"

Kojou looked back at Sensai Aiba's intimidating face as he doubted his own ears.

He could not immediately comprehend what was being said to him. It was almost like what the father of a lovely bride would say to her groom. But though he wondered if this was a joke, Sensai's look was far too serious for that.

"Er, um… What do you mean by that…? What about what Asagi thinks?"

Don't tell me he's gonna make me marry Asagi out of the blue, Kojou nervously thought. Given Sensai's connections and influence, making that happen was probably child's play.

Sensai's expression did not change as he continued in a quiet, conversational tone.

"Someday you, too, will understand, but my daughter was born carrying a somewhat troublesome destiny... In one sense, as much as your own, if not more."

"Asagi's...destiny?"

Kojou, affected by Sensai's calm demeanor, regained a little of his composure. However, no matter how he thought it over, he couldn't understand the meaning of Sensai's words. Asagi was an ordinary human being, unlike Kojou and Yume. It wasn't like she was an Attack Mage like Yukina and Natsuki, either.

When he thought harder about it, the only thing that stood out in his mind was how terrorists had once abducted Asagi because of her preeminent hacking abilities. And yet, he sensed something like unshakable conviction from Sensai's eyes.

"Therefore, if the time comes that Asagi needs you...will you stand by her side?"

Sensai spoke in a tone full of confidence, almost like a prophet.

Kojou may not have known what he truly wanted, but long before, the answer to that question was set in stone.

"Well, of course."

"I thank you, Kojou Akatsuki." Sensai smiled, full of satisfaction. Then he suddenly put on his capable politician's face as he said, "Incidentally, I have two daughters. I understand you are the firstborn son of your family, but there is the option of entering my family via adoption. I wonder what your parents would think about that?"

"Huh? Adoption?"

So you are *talking about that,* thought Kojou, ferociously thrown for a loop. *What happened to Asagi's destiny and all that?!*

"I am a politician, after all, so it is about time for me to think about who will continue my legacy. Oh, there's nothing to worry about. The fame of the Fourth Primogenitor will serve very well in an election. And if you are interested in the world of politics, in time, I will mold you into a fine politician."

"Er, ah, right now I'm not really interested in that stu—"

"But fooling around with girls is a no-no. Just no. If you have female acquaintances besides Asagi, do sort that out as quickly as possible. I will provide whatever money you require."

"I told you I'm not into that stuff..."

With Kojou hesitant, Sensai endeavored to persuade him with the full force of his skilled politician's talent. But as the man did so, Kojou made a pained sound as something struck the back of his head. This was followed by a sharp blow that hit the tip of his nose.

"What are you two talking about?!"

"Oww... A-Asagi?!"

As Kojou moaned, putting a hand to his face, he saw Asagi posing with what looked like a whip. Her cheeks were as red as the sun floating over the horizon for the first time that year.

"Goodness, just when I wonder where you've run off to... Kojou, you don't need to humor anything Dad says to you!"

"Er, but as the head of a political party, the issue of a successor is rather—"

"Oh, shut up! Get him, Azar!"

"Nuoooo?!"

Asagi transformed into a beast tamer as she sicced her beloved dog on her own father. The giant boxer dog playfully bowled Sensai over right then and there. His dignity as a stern-faced politician evaporated into thin air.

"Kojou, you wanted to bring Himeragi home, right? Sumire got a car ready, so..."

Asagi pointed toward the Aiba residence's front door as she spoke. When Kojou looked, he saw Sumire escorting Yukina near the entrance to the garden. The look on Yukina's face was still a bit stiff, but her physical condition seemed to have improved.

That said, it had been an all-nighter for Kojou, and his physical energy was finally reaching its limits. He was concerned about Nagisa, but to maintain his ability to make rational decisions, among other things, he needed to go back home and rest for the time being.

"Sorry to make you go through all this trouble, Asagi. You were a big help."

"Oh, that's all right. I'm worried about Nagisa, too, you know."

Asagi waved dismissively, as if concealing a blush.

"I'll gather what info I can, so act calmly, will you? In particular, watch Himeragi so she doesn't run off and do something reckless. Also, take this."

"...Huh?"

"This is my spare smartphone. If you have this, you can talk straight to Mogwai. There's no guarantee he'll do what you tell him, but I thought you should have it in case it comes in handy."

"R-right."

With a hint of concern on his face, Kojou gazed at the garishly pink smartphone that was handed to him.

The model was unfamiliar, and the device had traces of being modified in all manner of ways. The only thing displayed on the screen was an avatar resembling a poorly sewn teddy bear. Of course, Kojou knew that Mogwai was extremely capable but felt deep down that he wasn't very trustworthy. All the same, his power was necessary to narrow down Nagisa's whereabouts.

"Keh-keh... It's a pleasure."

Whether aware of Kojou's gloom or not, Mogwai flashed a sarcastic smile.

5

The car Sumire Aiba had arranged for Kojou and Yukina was expensive and painted black. Unexpectedly, it was Sumire herself behind the wheel.

Apparently, she used to be a driver in Sensai's employ. According to her, right after Sensai's first wife passed away from illness, he fell into peril due to a trap laid by a political enemy, and while continually on the run, the two fell in love. Kojou didn't know how far to believe her tale, but Sumire's driving skills were the real deal.

Since marrying Sensai, she'd settled down as a proper politician's wife, but even then, she felt calmest when driving a car—or so Sumire asserted.

With those words as the foundation, she engaged in even friendlier chitchat than she had in her own home. She was particularly interested in knowing how Asagi, her stepdaughter, was doing in school. She also lobbed pointed questions about Kojou and Yukina's relationship.

Since Yukina was still holding her silence, staring somewhere in the sky above, it naturally fell to Kojou to answer those questions. Even in the early morning, the main thoroughfares were packed; Sumire looked like she was enjoying herself, but Kojou's mental energy was being whittled down bit by bit.

"—I am sorry to interrupt. But could you please bring us to Hill Number Six?"

The car was just crossing a familiar intersection when Yukina spoke, almost as if she'd suddenly remembered something. "*Ahem!*" went Sumire, strongly coughing at that instant.

It was not surprising this gave her pause. Hill No. 6 was the name of a special place on Island West. It was a row of lodging facilities catering to couples—in other words, a love-hotel district.

"Er, not for that. It's not like *that* at all. Hill Number Six is where the Lion King A—erm, an acquaintance of Himeragi's is running a store. Right, it's kinda like an antique shop."

Kojou desperately explained away Sumire's misunderstanding.

Sorcery-wise, Hill No. 6, densely packed with special structures, had numerous magical blind spots. The Lion King Agency made use of that characteristic, laying down an office that served as a communications relay. To the naked eye, it looked like nothing more than a run-down antique shop, and at any rate, a special ward wiped the place from people's memories without any trace.

Yukina probably wanted to go there to get in touch with the Lion King Agency, but Sumire didn't know what Yukina intended.

"It's all right, don't worry. I'll keep it a secret from Asagi. It's good to be young…"

"I said it's not that!"

Sumire's excessive sympathy and consideration only backed Kojou farther into a corner. Certainly, having this exposed to Asagi would be more trouble than it was worth, but having Sumire misunderstand *that* much was a pain.

"Here is fine. Please stop the car."

Kojou was so nervous he didn't even notice that Yukina somehow seemed backed into a corner herself. When Sumire pulled the car over to the curb, Yukina politely gave her thanks and rushed out.

"Now then, I will wait here for about three hours. Take your time."

"What?! No, ah, please go home. It's bad for you to wait around in a place like this."

Kojou shook his head in surprise at Sumire's excessively generous offer. Whatever the circumstances, he certainly couldn't put her through that much trouble. Besides, Kojou couldn't judge whether it was all right to let Sumire, a civilian, come into contact with the Lion King Agency.

However, it seemed Sumire read Kojou's intent differently.

"In other words, three hours will not be sufficient for your activities…"

"What do you mean, activities?!"

"I'm kidding. You have your reasons, don't you? But please try not to make Asagi cry too much," Sumire said with a mischievous smile.

Sly like a fox, thought Kojou as he sighed. He couldn't tell at all just how much she understood. But he did grasp that she was a woman made of far sterner stuff than her appearance let on. He could understand why Sensai Aiba had chosen her as his wife.

"Go on ahead."

"Sure." Kojou bowed his head as he got out of the car. "Sorry for the trouble."

Yukina was standing at a narrow intersection midway up the hill. Her lips were pursed, her expression was hard, and it felt like she'd lost her usual air of composure.

"Himeragi. What's up with Professor Kitty?"

Kojou made certain of his surroundings as he asked.

Professor Kitty was the nickname Kojou had arbitrarily assigned to Yukina's master. She was apparently a formidable Attack Mage, but Kojou had only met her through a cat serving as her familiar.

"…Wait, where was it? The Lion King Agency branch office was around here, wasn't it?"

"The ward's enchantment has been changed. Even I cannot decode it."

Yukina spoke in an almost monotone voice. Kojou realized that the very cold ring of her voice meant Yukina was angry. Apparently, the Lion King Agency involving Nagisa in something behind Yukina's back had really gotten under her skin.

"Then even you can't get in? Why'd they go out of their way to do that?"

"I do not know. However, if that was their intention—"

With that, Yukina suddenly moved a hand to the guitar case on her back. From the case, she drew out her silver spear in its folded form.

The spear's shaft slid forward, making a metallic clang as a three-pronged blade deployed. Even early in the morning with no sign of anyone close, Kojou was flabbergasted that Yukina was wielding her spear in the middle of the street.

"H-Himeragi?!"

"Stand back, senpai— Snowdrift Wolf!"

Yukina wildly swung the silver spear.

Her spear, called Demon-Purging Assault Spear Type Seven, aka Schneewaltzer, was a secret weapon of the Lion King Agency. It had the ability to nullify magical energy and rend any barrier asunder.

Naturally, this effect was fully functional against the aversion ward the Lion King Agency used to conceal its own branch office. After a *ting*, the ward was annihilated, leaving behind a sound like glass breaking as the look of the surrounding urban landscape changed. A tiny alley appeared, one they had somehow managed to miss until then. Within, they could see a run-down antique shop. It was the familiar branch office of the Lion King Agency.

"That was nuts…"

"It is an emergency."

Kojou exhaled, seeming beside himself, as Yukina, still brandishing the spear, replied bluntly.

Yukina's personality, serious to the point of excess, had a glaring flaw: She got *very* worked up about things. This rampage was the result. Even if the act was out of concern for Nagisa, it wasn't good. Kojou knew painfully well why Asagi had told him to keep Yukina from doing anything reckless.

When they finally reached the antique shop, Kojou put a hand on the door and listlessly shook his head.

"So they're closed… Figures."

It was six AM on New Year's Day. Of course, the door would be locked. The curtains over the windows were shut, so they couldn't peer inside the shop.

"I have to say, without Professor Kitty here, it really does look like a simple antique shop. That talk of it being a Lion King Agency branch office—that's not some kind of mistake, is it…?" Kojou said lightheartedly.

He didn't intend for his words to come off as a jab, but the instant Yukina heard them, she looked ready to burst into tears.

"Ugh...!"

Then she gripped her spear, turning its tip toward the door of the antique shop. She meant to break down the door. Realizing this, Kojou rushed to pin Yukina's arms behind her.

"H-Himeragi, wait! What exactly are you going to do after breaking into the shop?!"

"Senpai, please stay out of my way! Let go of me!"

"Just calm down, okay...? No point busting into the place if there's no one in there!"

"But...!"

"In the first place, ain't no way an antique shop is gonna be open at this hour on New Year's Day. Aren't the Lion King Agency employees out for the New Year's holiday? They work for the government, after all."

"They wouldn't be... At a time like this...!"

Yukina seemed mortified as her shoulders trembled.

It wasn't as if he couldn't understand her feelings of anger. On the mainland, part of the Lion King Agency was surely still at work under the name of the Sorcerous Disaster Commission. Besides, Yukina couldn't possibly accept that her superiors were taking the holiday off.

"You can't get in touch with the Lion King Agency HQ?"

"High God Forest is isolated from the outside world..."

"How about contacting other branch offices?"

"I...do not know how."

Yukina's voice became fainter with each question from Kojou. "I see," he murmured, sighing heavily. Though she had been granted the title of Sword Shaman, Yukina was on the outer edge of the organization. She hadn't been granted any way to gather information about the organization as a whole.

"Himeragi, their not telling you anything means the Lion King Agency wanted us thoroughly cut off from information. I mean, we only got ahold of Nagisa's photo through dumb luck. If it was just some sort of communications lapse, it doesn't explain why we can't get in touch with Kirasaka."

"...Senpai, how can you be so calm about this? The Lion King Agency might have involved Nagisa in some kind of dangerous incident for all we know!" Yukina reproached him.

Kojou shifted his gaze to the sky, looking conflicted, and said, "It's not that I'm calm about this. I didn't trust the Lion King Agency much to begin with, so them betraying me wouldn't be that shocking."

"Ngh…"

"Ah, nah, it's not like I ever doubted you, Himeragi." Kojou added the quick follow-up once he saw Yukina biting her lip and looking forlorn with a downcast gaze.

"But it's like Asagi told us before," he continued. "The Lion King Agency's actions aren't always just. Besides, you'll find factions and internal disputes in any large organization."

"…Internal disputes…?"

The Sword Shaman blinked in surprise. Apparently, Yukina, strait-laced to the bone, had never considered the possibility that the Lion King Agency contained people she could not trust.

"Himeragi, I'm saying that if there's a side of the Lion King Agency you've never seen, that's no reason for you to feel guilty. I don't know about Professor Kitty, but at the very least, I don't think Kirasaka would ever betray you."

"I… I suppose not…"

Yukina nodded with a frail look. It wasn't as if she'd put her feelings completely in order, but she did seem to accept that much. After all, it was far from established that the entire agency had betrayed her.

Then, with Yukina having regained her composure, her cheeks suddenly reddened as she looked up at Kojou and said, "Um, senpai. I'd be happy if you finally let go of me now…"

"…Huh?"

Hearing her words, Kojou belatedly remembered that he was still pinning Yukina's arms behind her. Yukina's body was delicate enough that the embrace had slipped from his mind, but for all that, she was unexpectedly soft, and her skin was gently and intimately pressed against his.

"Or rather, just where do you think you're touching…?"

"R-right… Sorry."

Hearing the ice in Yukina's voice, Kojou nervously pulled his hands away.

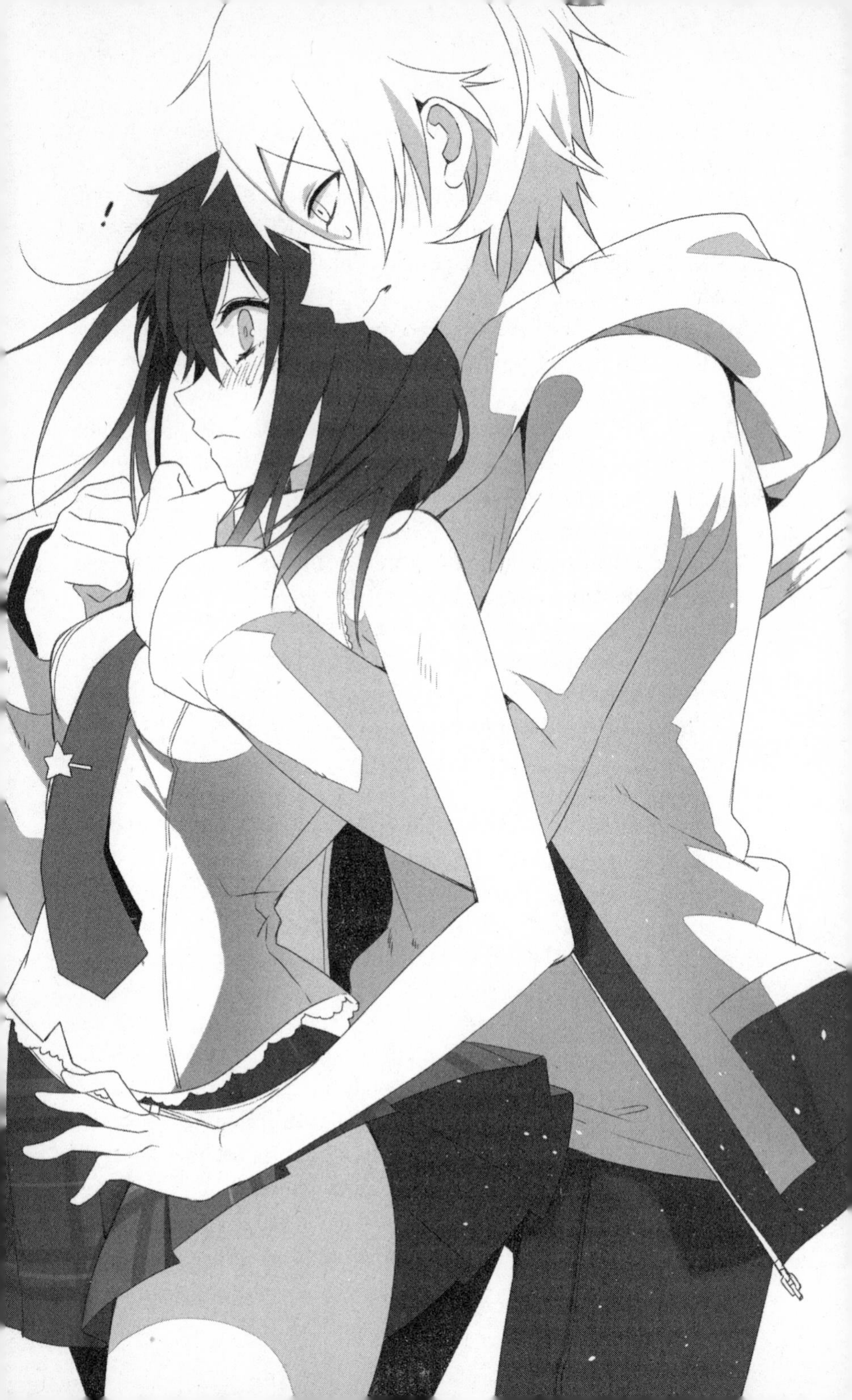
!

"No, it's fine. It was my fault to begin with…"

Once she had calmed down, Yukina put her clothes in order. Then she folded her spear and returned it to the guitar case.

"Well, setting all that aside, we still don't know what the Lion King Agency's goal is. No clues, either…"

Kojou murmured at his own expense, feeling stifled, as if walls were closing in around him.

He couldn't get in touch with Nagisa or Gajou. With the Lion King Agency shutting off information, they had no way of knowing what had happened at Kannawa Lake. Asagi said she'd check on things, but the information you could gather via the Net had its limits. Unlike Itogami Island, a man-made isle, the Kannawa Lake environs were still thick with nature, and virtually no electronic devices for Asagi to hijack.

What should we do? Kojou asked himself internally.

The next moment, in the middle of the road, early morning with no sign of anyone around, he heard the echo of a gentle voice:

"It would seem you are in distress, Fourth Primogenitor."

"—?!"

Kojou and Yukina simultaneously turned in the direction of the voice.

For the first time, she entered their sight—a slender figure standing with her back to the dazzling morning sun. Traditionally-styled, long, black hair trailed down her back, and she wore a similarly old-fashioned black sailor outfit. Even against the sun, her beauty was unmistakable, but because of her eyes, which seemed to look down on the entire world, her natural expression made her appear rather sinister.

"Kiriha Kisaki…!"

Yukina immediately raised her guard, reaching for the guitar case on her back. Kojou, too, lowered his center of gravity, adopting a posture for moving at any instant.

Kiriha Kisaki was a Priestess of the Six Blades of the Bureau of Astrology—an expert in anti-demonic beast combat. They employed the same techniques as the Sword Shamans of the Lion King Agency and the two professions were said to be opposite sides of the same coin.

About a month prior, she and Yukina had faced off against each other during the Blue Elysium incident.

The victor of that duel had not yet been decided. However, at that moment, Kojou didn't get the feeling they would be picking up where they left off. Nor was there any sign of Kiriha reaching toward the large tripod case she carried on her back.

"It's been a while, Yukina Himeragi. What an awful face. Are you aware that you look like an abandoned puppy?"

Kiriha looked back at the hesitant Yukina, trying to rub salt in her wounds. She wasn't attempting to pick a fight—it was just the only way she knew how to talk to other people.

"You want to know what the Lion King Agency is up to at Kannawa Lake, yes? Am I wrong?"

"And you know...?"

"Yes, of course. I can tell you if you'd like."

Kiriha looked back at the surprised Kojou, smiling sardonically.

The Bureau of Astrology she belonged to was a special agency under the umbrella of the Ministry of Home Affairs. Since their organizational objectives overlapped, they and the Lion King Agency's interests were frequently at odds—hence why they kept track of the Lion King Agency's movements.

"Really, I wanted to tell you much sooner, but you two were embracing so intimately, I just couldn't find it in me to interrupt."

"Wha—?! W-we were not!"

"That wasn't *embracing*, dammit!"

Kojou glared, with a red-faced expression that screamed *You were watching us?!* Kiriha smiled with indifference as she gazed at the pair's reactions.

"I do not mind telling you the truth, but our Bureau of Astrology and the Lion King Agency are at odds. Despite that, will you trust my words?"

"Just tell us already."

Kojou bared his fangs and pressed Kiriha to continue.

"If hearing the information isn't convenient for the Lion King Agency, you're the ones who benefit from giving it to us. In that sense, I'll trust you," Yukina said.

"I see. A sound decision." Kiriha nodded in a show of admiration.

She knew Kojou's objective. The Bureau of Astrology no doubt intended to use Kojou to hinder the Lion King Agency's actions. But that also meant Kiriha was certain Kojou would end up as the group's enemy.

"Very well, I shall tell you all that I know. Though I believe you will regret your decision…"

Kiriha stated her preamble with the crimson-dyed horizon at her back.

Such was how that fated day—a day upon which Kojou and Yukina would be faced with a difficult decision—began.

CHAPTER THREE
ESCAPE FROM THE DEMON SANCTUARY

1

It was noon when Kojou awoke.

Surprisingly, he'd slept rather well. Though he hadn't even been asleep three hours, his head was mysteriously clear. Perhaps it was that he knew what he had to do, and he had resolved to do it.

Kojou slipped out of bed, took a shower, and changed clothes. He changed into his Saikai Academy winter uniform, something he normally had little opportunity to wear. Rather than his blazer jacket, he wore a somewhat thicker parka in its place.

He didn't have much to pack. Aside from his house key, his cell phone and the modified smartphone Asagi had given him were the only devices he was bringing along. He didn't know what might happen, so it was best to travel as lightly as possible.

The problem was a lack of funds to buy necessary supplies in the field. The money Kojou kept on hand wasn't much to rely on.

Well, I can't change that, Kojou told himself as he headed to Nagisa's room.

Of course, the room was unoccupied. Nagisa was a neat freak, so her room was immaculate.

Without any hesitation, Kojou approached his little sister's desk and reached toward it.

"I was pretty sure she hid it over this way…"

As he thought, even amid her methodical cleaning, she had still taken the time to stash away a considerable amount of magazines and stickers. Among these, Kojou discovered a single brass key. Ever since she was little, Nagisa maintained a two-step system for retrieving anything important from the desk.

The diary hidden among the other things he removed tugged at his mind, but Kojou resisted the temptation and headed for a Western-style clothes closet. Nagisa had put a sturdy lock on her favorite closet. To the best of Kojou's knowledge, the item he was searching for rested within. But:

"What the heck is this?!"

When Kojou opened it, his eyes were greeted by assorted pairs of bras and panties stored within. Their designs and fabrics were completely different from the ones Nagisa normally wore. Apparently, this was underwear for "special occasions."

"She keeps *this* in her locked closet…?!"

Kojou grumbled as he rummaged through the contents. Though it went without saying, Kojou's objective was not his little sister's special underwear. He was searching for something else. Finally, after much labor, Kojou found the bank card and bank books he was looking for, hidden under a pair of panties.

"Well, I can get by as long as I have this, I guess."

Kojou selected one of the bank books from the pile and exhaled as he checked the remaining funds. There was 149,289 yen left over. He didn't know whether that was a lot for a high school student's life savings, but if he was thrifty, he'd have enough to get by.

"Sorry, Nagisa. I'm gonna be using this."

Giving a mental apology to his absent little sister, Kojou stuffed the bank card into his pocket. The next moment:

"…What are you doing, senpai?"

A voice cold enough to give Kojou chills stabbed into his back.

"Nuoa!" exclaimed Kojou, his body leaping into the air as he shifted his gaze toward the speaker. Yukina, her presence imperceptible, was standing behind Kojou with a scornful expression coming over her. She must have gotten out of bed and rushed over in a hurry; she was dressed in light gray pajamas with a hood. The hood had animal ears sewn onto it. From a distance, she looked like some kind of cartoon character.

"H-Himeragi… What are you doing here…?!"

"Nagisa gave me her spare key for times like these."

As Yukina said this, she dangled a familiar-looking key holder in front of him. Apparently, Yukina had used the key to let herself in through the front door.

"What do you mean, times like these?!"

"I believe you have been caught red-handed. Do you require further explanation? I placed a seal on Nagisa's drawers that responds when someone opens them."

As Kojou stood in front of the drawers, Yukina turned her lens toward him and snapped the camera's shutter. Certainly, based on that visual evidence alone, it looked like Kojou was rummaging through Nagisa's underwear.

Kojou vigorously shook his head and insisted, "No! You've got it all wrong! I wasn't looking for Nagisa's underwear and stuff, I was looking for my bank card! She confiscated it and said if I kept hold of it, I'd use it too much!"

Kojou thrust the bank ledger in front of Yukina. The majority of the money in his account was from his part-time job during middle school. The rest was scraps of money he'd received from cleaning Mimori's lab and running errands for Gajou, compulsory labor that was "helping out" in name only.

Kojou had meant to use it for club outing expenses, but the money had gone unused after he quit the basketball club.

"…What do you intend to do with that money?"

Yukina continued to hold the camera up as she inquired in a suspicious tone.

"Uh," went Kojou. His words caught for a moment before he said, "Er, you know, right—it's New Year's, so I figured I'd get myself a present. Go wild bargain hunting with the first sales of the New Year."

"Bargain hunting in your winter school uniform…?"

Kojou remained frozen, cold sweat coursing while under Yukina's half-lidded glare. He'd tried his best to be subtle, paying attention to minute details in preparation for his plan so that Yukina, his watcher, would not notice, but being foiled because he snuck into the place Nagisa kept her special underwear was well beyond his expectations.

"You intend to go to the mainland, senpai?"

"Well, yeah."

Kojou sighed in resignation and nodded. Yukina's eyebrows twitched upward in visible displeasure.

"Secretly, without one word to me?"

"Well, you'd stop me, Himeragi."

Kojou acted like he was starting over as he spoke. Yukina stared at him with a dead serious look and said:

"I suppose so. After all, you are a vampire primogenitor, senpai. Even if you are tolerated inside a Demon Sanctuary, I believe you walking around doing as you please on the mainland would be a major issue. I could not possibly overlook it."

"Er...you can't, ah, let that slide somehow?"

"I cannot."

"Figures..." Kojou twisted his lips.

"Good grief." Yukina sighed as she glared at him.

"In the first place, how do you intend to get there from Itogami Island? I take it you have not forgotten that a Demon Sanctuary is obliged to conduct strict medical checks on anyone entering or departing? The fact that you are the Fourth Primogenitor would be exposed for certain."

"Ah...well, I suppose you're right about that."

Kojou gloomily ran a hand through his hair. The practical means to get off Itogami Island, an isolated isle, were limited to air and sea. On top of that, every airport and harbor was garrisoned by an Island Guard unit protecting the border against unregistered demons. As a resident of a Demon Sanctuary, Kojou knew very well how difficult it would be to slip past their surveillance.

"That's why I was hoping Natsuki could deal with that somehow."

"Ms. Minamiya...?"

Yukina blinked in apparent surprise, perhaps finding Kojou's reply an unexpected one.

"Would it not be difficult for even Ms. Minamiya to waive your medical check, senpai?"

"Ahh, er, that's not really what I meant."

As an exceptional federal Attack Mage, Natsuki had a lot of pull with the Gigafloat Management Corporation—but that only mattered within

Itogami Island's borders. Letting Kojou, the Fourth Primogenitor, off the island without prior arrangements was surely beyond even Natsuki's power. In the first place, he had a hard time imagining the arrogant Natsuki playing politics and pulling strings behind the scenes.

"Clearing the exit inspection is a lot of trouble, but covering for me if I leave the island should work, right? So I was thinking Natsuki could give me a little teleport inside of an airplane or something."

"...In other words, you intended to stow away?"

Yukina put her hands on her hips in visible exasperation. Kojou gravely nodded.

"Depending on circumstances, I suppose you could read it like that."

"I do not believe there is any other way to read it..."

"Well, it's an emergency, so it can't be helped! I'd use a less suspicious way if I could!"

Finally, Kojou lost his cool as he shouted. However, Yukina's follow-up did not relent.

"Even if you did manage to reach the mainland, what did you plan to do when it was time to come back?"

Yukina calmly persisted with her questions, almost like she was offering guidance to a young child. Customs inspections when entering Itogami Island were far stricter than those when leaving.

"I figured I'd work that out as I went along." Kojou puffed his chest out in obvious desperation.

Yukina put a hand to her temple as if she was getting a headache and said, "You didn't think it through at all, did you?"

"Well, worst case, I thought I could tell them I'm a vampire, and then they'd boot me back to Itogami Island anyway."

"Are you really all right with that, senpai? That would expose your true nature to Nagisa."

"Th...that so...?"

Well that's bad, thought Kojou, clutching his head. Though a resident of a Demon Sanctuary, Nagisa had a severe case of demonophobia. If she knew Kojou was a vampire, it would surely bring her an incredible amount of anguish. That would render Kojou going all the way to the mainland pointless.

"Goodness... You lost sight of such an important thing because you tried to go to the mainland without one word to me."

"Er, I don't really think the two are related..."

Kojou weakly rebutted the gnawing irrationality of Yukina's reasoning. "*Ahem*," went Yukina, clearing her throat before she continued.

"At any rate, I will change clothes and be right back, so please wait right here!"

"Wait... Why?"

"You are heading to Ms. Minamiya's residence to ask her to help you stow away, yes?"

Yukina, apparently mystified, inclined her head slightly as she posed the question. To Kojou, Yukina's reaction was the far greater surprise. Hadn't she come to stop him...?

"Wait, Himeragi, don't tell me you plan on coming with me...?"

"The mission assigned to me by the Lion King Agency is to be your watcher. Naturally, if you go to the mainland, I must go with you, senpai. That is what a watcher is for."

"Er, but you said earlier you couldn't overlook this..."

"That was in the sense of 'I cannot allow you to go out of my sight'..."

Yukina pushed her chest out in pride as she spoke. Now that Kojou calmly thought it over, Yukina hadn't told him not to go—not once. She'd simply been exasperated at the sloppiness of Kojou's plan.

"Himeragi..."

Kojou subconsciously averted his eyes from Yukina, who had strongly declared *Let's go together*. Then he put a hand over his face. He seemed like he was overcome with emotion, desperately holding back tears.

"P-please do not get so sentimental about it, senpai. This is for Nagisa's sake, so I am tolerating your illegal conduct because there is no other choice—nothing more! And it was wrong for you to try to leave the island without telling me in the first place!"

For her part, Yukina was getting nervous from Kojou's unexpectedly dramatic reaction. Naturally, even she hadn't expected Kojou would be so overjoyed.

However, Kojou did not seem quite ready to burst into tears, shaking his head with a conflicted look as he said:

"Ah, no…it's not that…"

"Huh?"

"No, it's— Now that I'm thinking clearly, your outfit's just… *Pfft…*"

Kojou, finally reaching the limits of his endurance, burst into laughter that made his shoulders tremble.

Yukina was wearing hooded pajamas with animal ears. There was a little tail coming out of the back of her pants, too. That they'd been having a serious conversation while she was dressed like that was too much for Kojou to take.

Then Yukina's cheeks went crimson with a blush as she realized why Kojou was laughing.

"…?! No, ah, th-these are pajamas from when Nagisa bought some together for the sleepover we had recently… Th-they're cute, aren't they…?!"

"Yeah, those mouse ears suit you really well, Himeragi."

"*Wolf* ears!!"

"Pffft…!"

The design of Yukina's hood, which looked like a field mouse's ears no matter how hard he looked, cracked Kojou up once more. Yukina's cheeks puffed up as she glared at Kojou for laughing at her favorite pair of pajamas.

"What are you laughing at, stupid senpai?!"

Such was the lack of tension on the eve of their departure.

2

"This will sting a little."

At a ticket window smelling of antiseptic, a nurse stuck a needle into Asagi's arm to draw blood. The nurse immediately put the blood she gathered into an analyzer, and the screen displayed that Asagi's cells were human.

"Yes, no problem at all. Now then, please enter your name and Itogami City Citizen ID Number and advance to the blue ticket window."

Asagi sighed slightly as she took a form from the nurse.

She was in the domestic airline departure lobby of Itogami Central Airport. With the paperwork for boarding her flight and her luggage safety check already complete, she was currently undergoing her exit inspection. For a resident of Itogami Island, a Demon Sanctuary, getting off the island required more annoying formalities than what other people typically faced when visiting foreign countries.

"It's a big fuss like this every time. I get that we're a Demon Sanctuary, so that's just how it is, but…"

Asagi complained to no one in particular as she headed for the next ticket window.

A man with a face reminiscent of Buddha sat in the booth on the other side of thick, acrylic glass. The clerk's eyes perused Asagi's document, staring at her with an unenthused look as he said, "Asagi Aiba. Boarding alone?"

"Yes."

She managed to swallow the words *Isn't that obvious?* and kept them from leaving her throat as she smiled amiably toward him. The clerk didn't even grin.

"Destination?"

"Tokyo. To visit my older sister attending university in the city."

"Any symptoms such as fever, nausea, diarrhea?"

"None whatsoever."

Asagi continued her plain replies to the clerk's businesslike questions. Either way, these questions were standard formalities straight out of the rule book. But…

"Any cases of a vampire drinking your blood within the last three months?"

"Huh?!"

Asagi unwittingly let out an odd voice when the clerk's words took her by surprise.

The clerk shifted a cool gaze toward Asagi and said:

"If something comes to mind, please proceed to ticket window number four for reexamination."

"Ah, er, no. None whatsoever!"

"……"

Asagi's oddly nervous denial made the clerk stare at her with a suspicious look. However, he did not particularly pursue the matter, and Asagi made it out with a stamp on her exit permit.

This meant the annoying formalities were now complete.

"Ugh… That one really made me sweat."

Asagi pulled her carry-on bag along as she headed toward the airport terminal. During that time, she heard an oddly human-sounding synthetic voice from inside her bag. It was Mogwai talking, helping himself to her smartphone's speaker.

"Keh-keh. To be blunt, that's very fortunate, ain't it? The Fourth Primogenitor's French-kissed you, but he hasn't been drinking your blood…yet."

"It was not a French kiss!! Wait, how do *you* know about our kiss?!"

Asagi's lips twisted painfully as she groaned aloud. Asagi had kissed Kojou right after being involved in a weird terror incident. At the time, Asagi had no idea Kojou was a vampire; that might be why she felt the true meaning of her kissing Kojou had become muddled.

"Keh-keh," Mogwai cackled, seemingly teasing her about that very part. *"But it sure is big of you, li'l miss, goin' all the way to the mainland for that Kojou guy's sake."*

"Hey, it's not like I'm doing this for Kojou. I really haven't seen my big sister in a while, too."

Asagi said it like she was bluffing. Asagi's older sister used going to university as an opportunity to leave Itogami Island, and she was currently living in the capital. Asagi hadn't had a chance to meet up with her in almost half a year.

"Besides, I hate being the only one out of the loop like I've been all this time. That idiot Kojou is no doubt agonizing over how to cross over to the mainland right this minute."

"Really, now?" Mogwai praised Asagi's prophetic words. *"I see."*

Given his protectiveness toward his little sister, Kojou would soon be saying *I'm going to the mainland to look for Nagisa.* When he did, Yukina, his watcher, would of course accompany him. In the name of sensible reasons like not wanting to cause her any trouble, it was guaranteed that they'd leave Asagi behind. *To hell with that,* thought Asagi.

She was worried about Nagisa, too, so she also deserved to know the truth. Besides, unlike Kojou, a vampire, Asagi could leave Itogami Island by legitimate means. All things considered, in Asagi's mind, searching for Nagisa was her responsibility.

She was well aware that there was significant risk in what she was doing, but since she knew that going in, she could take countermeasures against them.

"Er...huh? I was boarding on terminal number four, right...?"

Asagi suddenly stopped when she realized that the airport interior was strangely empty.

She understood that few people used the airport on New Year's Day, but this was like a ghost town. That even airport staff were few in number made the sight downright bizarre.

When she looked up at the electronic board, there was no particular sign of anything amiss, only a number of flight schedules and boarding gates being changed—a sight you would see at any airport.

In spite of that, Asagi instinctively felt that something was off in a way that only she could discern. Her intuition told her that some kind of hidden process lurked behind the giant system known as "the airport."

"Not good, li'l miss. It's the Island Guard."

Mogwai's laid-back warning came a moment after Asagi noticed the shift.

"What?!"

"Sixteen armed guardsmen split into three squads, moving through staff corridors. They'll surround you in one minute and forty seconds. You're definitely their target, li'l miss."

"You've gotta be kidding me! Escape route! Now!"

"Run to the stairway sixty meters straight ahead. Go down, and I'll lead you out. The rest is up to chance, but it should be better than stickin' around inside the building."

"Ughh! Why does this have to happen on New Year's morning?!"

Asagi picked up her carry-on bag and made a dash for the stairs.

Apparently, her current reality was filled with far more danger than she had imagined.

3

Natsuki Minamiya's residence was an eight-story building in Island West. By all appearances, it was a top-tier apartment building, with no expense spared on its construction. As rumor would have it, the entire building was Natsuki's private property, and she apparently used the entire topmost floor like her own private penthouse.

After heading up by elevator to the eighth floor, Kojou and Yukina were finally at the entrance to Natsuki's personal home.

"Asagi's place is pretty huge, but this is pretty up there, too…"

No longer bothering to be envious, Kojou felt pure admiration as he rang the doorbell. After a while, Astarte appeared in the corridor, apparently all dressed up for New Year's Day.

"Happy New Year."

The indigo-haired homunculus girl delivered a New Year's greeting in a voice low on inflection, reminding Kojou and Yukina that it was in fact January 1; they had practically forgotten.

"H-Happy New Year."

"Sorry to drop in on you, Astarte. We came to talk to Natsuki… Can we see her?"

They hastily bowed their heads, somehow feeling bashful as they replied that way.

When Kojou took the time to look up, he saw that the place was adorned with pine boughs, *kagami mochi*: a traditional New Year decoration featuring two *mochi* stacked atop one another with a bitter orange at the very top, and other decorations. That was something to be praised, but it wrecked his mental image of the residence of one of the world's few "witches."

"Affirmative."

Astarte remained emotionless as she turned her back on the pair. *Come this way* was likely the meaning of the gesture. Kojou and Yukina nodded to each other and stepped into Natsuki's residence.

Contrary to their expectations, the interior had simple furnishings. The walls and ceiling made heavy use of glass, which made the place look futuristic. The furniture placed within was small with low backs, perhaps to match the size of Natsuki's body. Because of this, it all felt like a dollhouse that had been meticulously decorated by a little girl.

Astarte led Kojou and Yukina to a broad, spacious dining room.

Atop a long table appropriate for a banquet hall was a line of deep chafing dishes filled with extravagant cooking. A foreign-looking woman in a long-skirted garment was carrying plates over to the table.

She was a female knight with a gallant face and short silver hair.

"Huh? Justina?"

"...Sir Kojou?! And Lady Sword Shaman?!"

Noticing Kojou and the others entering the room, she pressed her hands together in front of her chest, making a stereotypical ninja pose.

"Allow me, Interceptor Knight Kataya Justina of the Aldegian Knights of the Second Coming, to humbly state with delight to all of you congratulations upon greeting the New Year."

"Y-you, too."

Kojou and the others were a bit overwhelmed by Justina's grandiose greeting. It was typical of her to be oddly well versed in her knowledge about Japan, her favorite subject.

"Or rather, what are you doing at Natsuki's place, Justina?"

"Well you see, Attack Mage Minamiya conveyed a command from my liege, Her Highness the Royal Sister, to report in for New Year's greetings and to aid in the preparation of Japanese New Year's cooking."

"O-oh."

In other words, Natsuki was apparently making her work for free.

"Royal Sister must mean Kanase. Oh yeah, she's living at Natsuki's place, too, isn't she...?"

"That is correct."

Justina affirmed Kojou's murmur.

Kanon, a victim of the Faux-Angel incident, was placed under Natsuki's guardianship in the aftermath. Appearances aside, Natsuki was quite attentive to the needs of others, perhaps as one might expect of a teacher.

Additionally, together with Kanon, there was one more resident living at the apartment.

"Oh, Kojou and Yukina are here?"

Climbing onto the tablecloth and addressing Kojou and Yukina extremely casually was a beautiful oriental doll not quite thirty centimeters tall. This was what was left of Nina Adelard, the Great Alchemist of Yore, who was more than two hundred and seventy years old. Due to particular circumstances, she had lost the majority of her body, reforming her flesh with what little liquid-metal remained; Kanon was looking after her.

"What brings you here? Perhaps you come bearing New Year's gifts for me, your elder?"

Nina posed the question with a pompous tone, even though her social position was closest to that of *pet*.

Kojou flippantly waved a hand to her and said, "No need for a show of vanity. It's not like I look to you *or* Natsuki for dignity from my elders."

"Wha—?! Why you... You will regret insulting me, the Great Alchemist of Yore. I'll have you know, with the proper materials, I can create any amount of coinage that I please...!"

"Ain't that fool's gold?! And I can't trust your alchemy. Don't make me say it again," Kojou said, annoyed while Nina had tried to salvage her pride.

Nina was certainly an excellent alchemist, but because she had lived so long, her grasp on common sense was gradually weakening. The substances she could create via alchemy came at a high cost in materials, and in the first place, there was little need for alchemy in the modern era, making it a fairly useless skill set.

As Nina sulked from having this pointed out to her, they heard a new, gentle voice from behind Nina.

"Happy New Year, Yukina. And Akatsuki, too."

Entering from the kitchen and carrying a tray of rice cakes cooked with vegetables was a small-statured, silver-haired, blue-eyed girl. It was Kanon Kanase wearing a long-sleeved kimono. The fabric was blue and embroidered with silver flower patterns, matching her hair and eye colors extremely well.

Yukina rushed over to Kanon, taking the tray that Kanon had been awkwardly carrying.

"Happy New Year, Kanon... Are you all right?"

"S-sorry about that. I am not accustomed to these clothes, so it is difficult to move in them."

"Yes, but they're really cute."

"Astarte has one of her own. Miss Justina asked us... She said she wanted to see us in them."

Kojou gazed at Yukina and Kanon continuing their harmonious conversation when he felt a faint ache in his chest. Nagisa got along well

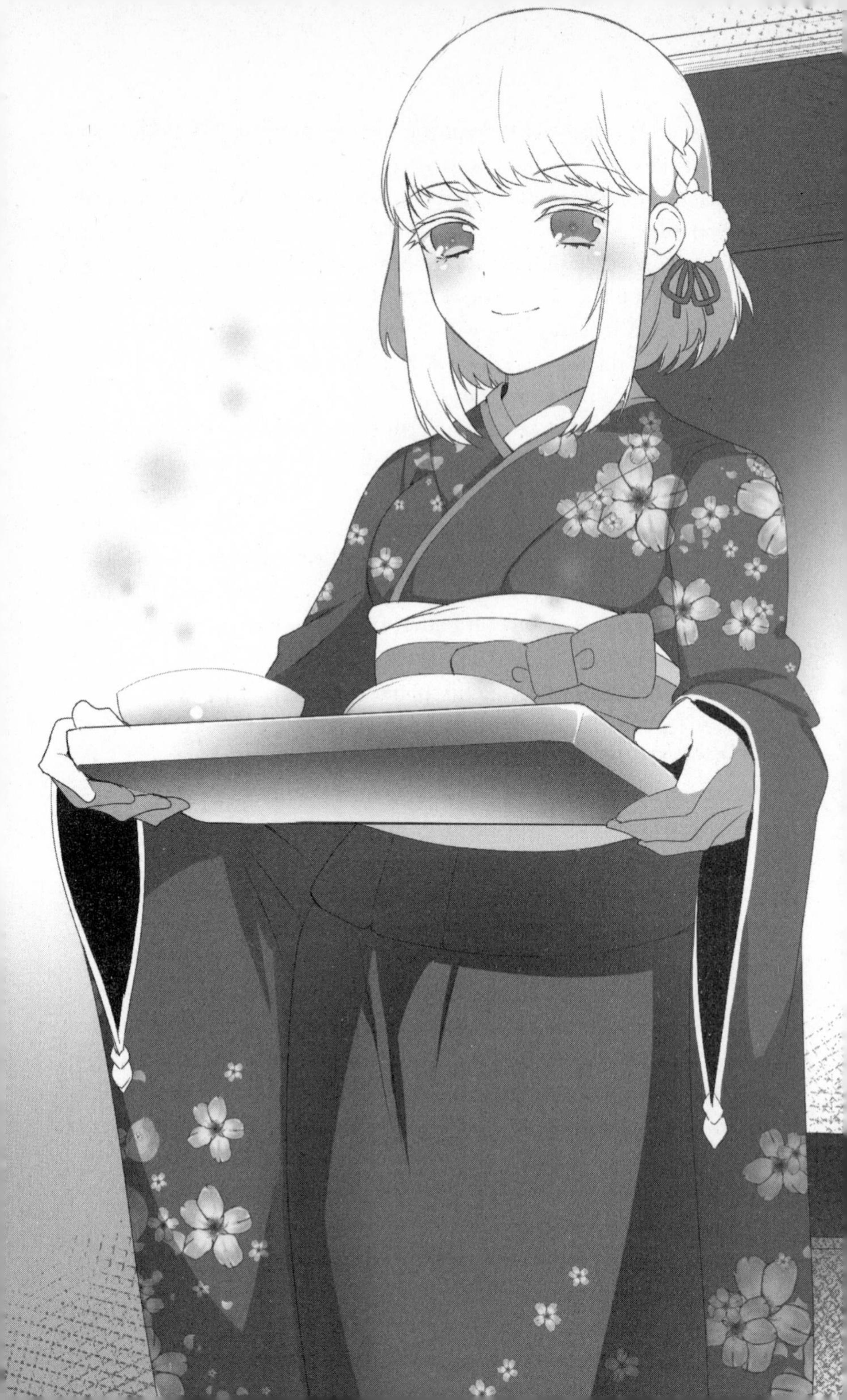

with both of them. He thought that if Nagisa was there, she'd be joining in, making the conversation far more boisterous.

But that scene wouldn't become a reality until Nagisa came home safe and sound.

"...Did Kanase and the others make this?" Kojou asked, staring at the platters of rich food on the table.

Kanon gave a charming smile as she nodded and said, "Yes. Akatsuki, Yukina, please have some if you'd like."

"Really? You're a lifesaver! Come to think of it, I haven't had a single bite since the year began."

Kojou made a strained smile as he recalled that his own stomach was empty. It might not have been the purpose of their visit, but a guy still had to eat.

"Please wait a moment. I shall prepare the cutlery at once."

With those words, Justina headed toward the kitchen. Yukina watched Justina's back as she left, seeming a little unable to calm down when she said:

"Is it really all right? I feel bad imposing all of a sudden like this..."

Nina, the most useless-seeming person there, replied with a tone that somehow sounded haughty when she said, "There is no need for concern. While we were engaged in trial and error, we cooked a tad too much."

"Trial and error...?"

The alchemist's nonchalant murmur made Kojou gulp as an instinctive feeling of unease came over him. Besides Nina, a liquid metal lifeform, there was a soldier from the Northern European kingdom of Aldegia, a royal girl raised in a convent, and a homunculus girl—not a single one seemed appropriately learned in the art of traditional Japanese cuisine.

Can anything those girls cooked really be considered proper New Year's dishes? wondered Kojou, full of doubt.

Heedless of Kojou's anxiety, Kanon put the New Year's dishes onto plates, then offered them to Kojou and the others. Yukina and Astarte were already seated; he couldn't just say *I don't wanna* at that point. Feeling pushed by a wordless, coercive force at his back, Kojou sat at the table as well.

"Th-this is…"

Now that he was seriously looking at the food at close range, Kojou felt even more conflicted. Certainly, by appearance, the food *resembled* a traditional New Year's meal. However, that which had been served clearly differed in several respects.

There was an aroma of steamed vegetables and rice cakes wafting around the bowl, and besides that, the scent of consommé.

Nina spread open a department store New Year's cookbook as she confessed up front, "I looked at the recipe and followed it as closely as I could. It may differ somewhat from pure Japanese New Year's cooking, but pay that no heed."

When Kojou timidly brought the food to his mouth with chopsticks, he groaned as its powerful spiciness seemed to scorch his throat.

"Well, I pay it heed! Why the hell did you put chili beans into New Year's cooking?!"

"Hm. Originally, beans were considered a very hardy food, so I thought them an indispensable ingredient in New Year's cuisine. It was my hope that their hardiness might extend to the whole year."

"Black soybeans and chili beans are completely different foods, you know! Well, not that it isn't tasty or anything!"

As Kojou spoke, he brought a rice cake with a consommé taste to his lips. Meanwhile, Yukina wore an odd expression as she put a food resembling a rolled omelet into her mouth.

"Is this…roll cake?" she asked.

"Yes. I learned to make sweets at the abbey, so it became my specialty."

"R-right, it's delicious."

A broad smile came over Kanon as Yukina conveyed her impressions with an odd look.

Kojou continued to eat silently. The New Year's cooking feint had thrown him off, but if you treated it like creative, slightly oddball cooking, it actually wasn't half bad.

"You've got Mont Blanc instead of sweet potatoes and chestnuts, but that's no big d—*Gnhh?!*"

Just when he'd gotten used to the mysterious cooking, carelessly lowering his guard, the instant Kojou reached his chopsticks toward a new plate, he covered his mouth and choked.

"Wh-what's that smell?!"

The beautifully decorated plate had food on it closely resembling pickled *kohada* millet. The fish went by different names as it increased in size, and if it was associated with anything, it certainly was to New Year's cooking.

However, the pungent stench intensely permeating Kojou's nostrils was clearly not from the warm, gentle cooking he was used to.

"This is salted herring, a traditional food of the Kingdom of Aldegia, my native soil. It is fermented via a strict two-stage process to add to the taste," Justina explained with a proud expression.

"Wait a… You're not telling me this is *that* pickled herring, considered, like, the smelliest food the world over…"

Kojou was gasping, tears streaming down his cheeks due to the extreme odor.

He could perfectly appreciate how Justina, a native of Northern Europe, would think of pickled fish as "cooking," but the stimulus was just too much for Kojou. Even if that would not have once been the case, becoming a vampire meant Kojou's senses were sharper than in the past.

"It is delicious."

"I was surprised to learn that there were commonalities between east Asian New Year's dishes and local Northern European cuisine."

Ignoring Kojou's agonized moans, Justina and Nina dug into the herring, broken apart from fermenting, with broad satisfaction. Though Kojou had his doubts that Nina, a liquid-metal life-form, could properly taste to begin with.

"Well, if you're happy with it, that's just great," he said, resigned.

Then Kojou shifted his eyes toward the still-empty seat. Normally, Natsuki would be sitting in that chair, but there was no sign of her in the dining room.

"Astarte, where's Natsuki…?"

"Unclear. I have received a command to the effect of *Make the two of them wait—give them dinner or something.*"

"Wait, Natsuki *told* you to do this?!"

Kojou exclaimed in shock as he gazed at the feast laid out before him. It wasn't like she had other guests, so why had Natsuki ordered her to kill time? *What's going on here?* thought a bewildered Kojou.

He then cleared off his plate with great haste, bowing his head to Astarte as he said, "Sorry, but I don't have a lot of time. Can't you just show us to Natsuki somehow or other?"

The atypical seriousness of Kojou's demeanor made Astarte hesitate. Her pale-blue eyes wavered.

"...Accepted." Her voice came slowly and quietly.

Kojou's and Yukina's faces met, and the two simultaneously rose to their feet.

"...Akatsuki?"

Kanon, noticing the tense expressions on their faces, murmured with unease.

"Hmm," said Nina, narrowing her eyes, her interest apparently piqued. That was when Justina, right next to them at the time, abruptly vanished from the dining room.

4

Natsuki received Kojou and others in her so-called reception room, which was actually nothing more than a wide, empty space.

It was a dimly lit room lacking even a window. The vast interior, larger than a Saikai Academy classroom, contained only a single antique chair. Aside from a solitary light, there were no fixtures of any kind. Glossy walls, seemingly made of obsidian, surrounded the room, lending it a cold, imposing air.

"What is it, Kojou Akatsuki? Come to give your homeroom teacher a New Year's gift?"

Natsuki, who seemed somehow small in the chair, made a wry, sarcastic smile as she spoke. Kojou shook his head and said:

"Hey, give it a rest. And Nina said that to me just earlier."

"What, then? Surely you have not come to continue your extra lessons?"

"Well, not that exactly, but I did come to ask something of you."

"Hmm?"

Turning back to see a rare look of seriousness on his face, for once, Natsuki rested her chin on her hand and motioned as if to say *Out with it already*. Kojou quietly steadied his breathing and spoke aloud:

"I want to go to the mainland. Please help me."

"You need a visa from the government for that."

Natsuki's reply was immediate and blunt.

"The issuance fee is thirty-three hundred yen. However, applicants must be registered as demons. It would expose you as an unregistered demon. You don't mind?"

"I'm not talking about that! I came to ask you because there ain't time for red tape!"

Kojou replied gruffly. Naturally, Natsuki had seen through his nervousness from the very beginning, and yet, she'd still evaded the question, which made Kojou's irritation all the greater.

"For you, waivin' the inspection and getting us to the mainland is simple, right?"

"Even if that was the case, I do not believe I have any duty to go that far for the likes of you."

"What if someone's life is at stake?"

Speaking those words, Kojou thrust his smartphone toward Natsuki. It was the picture Nagisa had taken of the magic circle.

Natsuki's delicate, doll-like eyebrows rose a few, precious millimeters.

But Yukina replied to Natsuki's question with a question of her own: "What is that?"

"Do you know of Kannawa Lake?"

Natsuki indifferently shifted her gaze toward Yukina, seemingly searching for the point of the question.

"...An artificial lake in Tangiwa of the Kansai region, currently well-known as a tourist destination."

"Yes."

Yukina took a photocopy of a newspaper story out of her jacket pocket. It was an old story—from more than forty years ago, according to the date. This was what Kiriha Kisaki of the Bureau of Astrology had handed to Yukina.

"On the current Kamioda Dam site rested a single village—a tiny settlement with a population of less than three hundred."

"So the village sank to the bottom of that lake, sacrificed for the dam. Tragic, but a common enough tale," Natsuki said, her tone calm as she crossed her legs in a show of tedium.

Yukina nodded vaguely and said, "I suppose it is. However, it was not the construction of the lake that was the demise of the village. The village vanished three years before the dam was completed."

"Why is that?"

"Because all the residents at the time disappeared, not leaving a single trace behind."

At Yukina's emotionally restrained words, Natsuki displayed clear interest for the first time.

"The cause?"

"I do not know. Perhaps the cause truly is unknown, or they have simply not divulged it to the public. However, this sunken village—old Kamioda Village—had a research facility from a corporation known as Saiki Shamanics."

"Shamanics... So a maker of enchanted devices? I have not heard the name. They went bankrupt?" Natsuki deduced.

"Yes."

In an odd coincidence, Saiki Shamanics went bankrupt the same year that Kamioda Dam was completed. At the time, all records of the proprietors and employees had been erased, without a single hint as to their whereabouts. The reason for it having gone bankrupt remained unknown.

"But that is odd. Why build a research facility in a backwater place like that?"

Natsuki prompted in a tone that did not sound particularly pleased.

"From this point onward is merely conjecture, but Kamioda District has a wreck from a crashed military aircraft. Additionally, I wondered if the cargo it was carrying might have included a powerful enchanted object."

"Military aircraft? A plane from the last great war?"

"Yes."

"So they went out of their way to build a facility to research that? These fetishes must have been quite a big deal."

"I suppose so. However, would it then be too great a stretch to wonder if that enchanted object was also responsible for the disappearance of the villagers? Or perhaps Kamioda Dam itself was constructed to seal it away?"

"Not bad as conspiracy theories go, but not a very convincing one. What enchanted object would be so great as to require a man-made reservoir weighing sixty-five thousand tons to seal it?" Natsuki quipped.

"How about a relic dating back to The Cleansing?" Yukina replied, annoyed.

"Keh," went Natsuki, smiling. "These are events over forty years ago in either case."

"However, if there was a factor that could activate the relic—"

"Nagisa Akatsuki?"

Yukina's voice, speaking at an increasingly rapid pace, was cut off by Natsuki's single utterance. The Sword Shaman's expression twisted into shock.

"Eh…?!"

"The Cleansing. Certainly, that field was Gajou Akatsuki's specialty. Furthermore, Nagisa Akatsuki has opened the seal of a Cleansing-era ruin once before."

"Why… Why do *you* know about that, Natsuki…?!" Kojou was just as surprised as Yukina.

Natsuki had no reason to suddenly bring up his sister's name at that particular moment—not unless she'd known the entire circumstances of her situation from the very beginning.

"So how did you two get information that the Lion King Agency was covering up? Through the Bureau of Astrology?"

As Kojou and Yukina stood rooted to the spot, Natsuki, as cold as ice, stared at them.

That was when Kojou finally understood. Someone had leaked information to Natsuki before he and Yukina had arrived. There was only one person Kojou knew who could have done so.

"Don't tell me that Kisaki chick came to meet you, too?"

"Just before the two of you arrived."

Natsuki bluntly confirmed his suspicions. In other words, Natsuki had known their objective from the very beginning.

"Say that first, geez! You didn't need to make us waste time tryin' to explain!" Kojou shouted fervently.

A smile came over Natsuki as she shook her head. "That is not so. Now

I know what that little Bureau of Astrology girl whispered into your ears."

"Whispered into our ears...?"

"The interests of the Bureau of Astrology and the Lion King Agency are at odds, yes? Then, what made you want to believe that shady-looking girl? Do you have any proof that what she says is true?"

"This photo *is* the proof. I stumbled onto data left from Nagisa's smartphone, but Asagi's the one who gathered this evidence. The Bureau of Astrology had nothing to do with it."

"Aiba did? Meddling in other people's business..."

Kojou felt a slight crack emerge in Natsuki's expression, triumphant up to that point.

Natsuki was an excellent Attack Mage. If it was purely a sorcery-related incident, even Yukina would yield to a simple explanation on her part. Yukina, honest to the core, would mentally waver and weaken, for Natsuki's experience far exceeded her own.

However, that was not so where electronic data was concerned. On Itogami Island, Asagi was second to none when it came to electronic warfare. With Asagi vouching that it was the real deal, there was no mistake that the image was the literal truth. It was that truth that had underpinned Kojou's and Yukina's willingness to take Kiriha's information at face value.

"Well, fine. Whether you're worried or not, your little sister is with Gajou Akatsuki, yes? You heading off will only make things more complicated. Leave this to the adults."

Natsuki, giving up on glossing the matter over, shifted to brusquely persuading Kojou and Yukina.

Though Natsuki's words were of little comfort to the primogenitor, she did have a point. It was Gajou who'd taken Nagisa off Itogami Island, and he had a solid record earned from wandering through a number of battlefields. Under normal circumstances, trusting Gajou to handle it would be the best plan.

"It'd be a hell of a lot easier if I could."

However, Kojou promptly declined Natsuki's suggestion. His eyes betrayed his nervousness and fear—the look of someone backed into a corner.

"Anything else, fine, but a relic from The Cleansing? No. That's way out of his league. Besides, Dad's not the one who set things up this time. I've got a bad feeling about this."

Spurred on by unease he could not easily put into words, Kojou fiercely shook his head.

Kiriha Kisaki hadn't given Kojou and Yukina all that much information. She'd merely raised the possibility that there was an enchanted object, apparently a legacy from The Cleansing, sunken at the bottom of the lake; and that a number of years prior, the Lion King Agency had expressed interest in that enchanted object. Also, that at the same time as Nagisa's visit, the Sorcerous Disaster Commission, the Lion King Agency's window to the government, had gone into motion...

Apparently, the Bureau of Astrology had yet to learn that Kamioda District had been sealed off by the Self-Defense Forces. However, for Kojou, the words *relic of The Cleansing* were reason enough.

In times past, within the ruin of a Demon Sanctuary in the Mediterranean, it was Kojou and Nagisa encountering such a relic of The Cleansing that had resulted in Nagisa being grievously injured, and Kojou and others entwined in checkered fates of their own.

Now, Nagisa was coming into contact with a relic of The Cleansing once more.

Just imagining that made Kojou's fear so great that it seemed sufficient to crush his heart.

"So please, Natsuki. Lend me your strength."

Kojou pleaded with Natsuki with such force, he seemed ready to prostrate himself at any moment.

However, an even plainer revealed that she had not been swayed in the slightest.

"I refuse."

"Why?!"

"Do I require a reason to stop a pupil from engaging in illegal activities?"

Natsuki's voice, completely bereft of warmth, thoroughly slammed into Kojou.

Then he instinctively understood.

No matter how many words Kojou might expend, Natsuki would

not budge an inch. It had nothing to do with her being his homeroom teacher; Natsuki had some other reason for stopping Kojou from escaping Itogami Island.

Perhaps that was not something of Natsuki's own will.

Behind Natsuki the Attack Mage loomed the Gigafloat Management Corporation. And the Corporation surely had reasons it did not want Kojou to leave the island. A reason why it did not want to let a precious pawn—a pawn called the World's Mightiest Vampire—slip through its fingers, just in case it was needed.

"I see. Understood."

"...Senpai?"

When Kojou spoke, seemingly stifling his emotions, Yukina stared at him in astonishment. She doubtless could not imagine Kojou would back down that easily.

"It's fine, Natsuki. It's my fault for saying selfish stuff without thinking about your position."

Kojou gently shook his head and turned his back on Natsuki.

"Wait, Akatsuki. Where do you think you're going?"

Natsuki knitted her brows as she glared at Kojou. However, he did not turn around, raising one hand as he said, "I'll find another way. Sorry to bother you."

"No, you won't."

Her voice was cruel.

That instant, Kojou's and Yukina's fields of vision wavered like ripples, and countless silhouettes appeared inside the broad reception room.

Kojou stared at them dumbfounded, unable to immediately process what was going on.

The armed guardsmen who had appeared surrounded Kojou and Yukina, guns trained upon them.

They were wearing anti-demon protective gear and wielding cutting-edge submachine guns: the gear of Island Guard special forces.

"Natsuki?!"

Kojou glared at the small-statured, doll-like witch as he shouted.

It was unthinkable for anyone save Natsuki to have teleported so many people at once. But that meant Natsuki had completely turned against them.

"You cannot be permitted to leave. You will behave yourself here, Akatsuki."

Natsuki joined the guardsmen as she spoke.

They were words of despair.

5

Eight armed guardsmen had appeared from the void. They were deployed in a pincer, hemming in Kojou and Yukina from the left and the right, and all their gun barrels were trained upon Yukina.

Realizing this, Kojou stopped in his tracks. Yukina's expression twisted in humiliation.

"Do not move, Akatsuki. Even a Sword Shaman of the Lion King Agency cannot evade submachine guns firing at six hundred rounds per minute. They are rubber bullets, but depending on where they hit, she may not be merely wounded." Natsuki's tone was frigid, indifferent.

Unlike Kojou, who possessed a vampiric body, Yukina was a flesh-and-blood human being. Even a single gunshot might inflict lethal injuries. Natsuki knew that and was using that to take Yukina hostage.

From Yukina's point of view, it was akin to an act of contempt—essentially declaring that her presence made the Fourth Primogenitor weak.

"Did you purposefully drag out the conversation to buy time so we might be surrounded?" Yukina asked, mortified, her voice quivering.

Having been in contact with Kiriha, Natsuki already knew that their objective was to leave Itogami Island. Therefore, she'd kept Kojou and Yukina trying to convince her while she called the Island Guard to her. Perhaps Kanon and the others' warm reception had also been to slow the pair down.

It was, all in all, an underhanded method that suited Natsuki poorly.

"Natsuki...why are you going this far...?!"

Kojou lamented, more in fiercely conflicted emotions than in anger. However, Natsuki's expression remained neutral and doll-like as she gazed at Kojou, raising her right hand.

"The transfer student on her own is one thing, but I cannot allow *you* to leave Itogami Island. You can take it easy in my world until things calm down. It is the least I can do."

"Ugh...!"

Kojou's breath caught as he felt incredible blows over his entire body. Silver chains shot out from the void and coiled around his whole body like sentient snakes.

"—I'll return you once winter break is over. Don't take this personally."

Behind Kojou, thin air contorted and shuddered as something like a haze emerged. That thin air became a gate through which one could see the contours of a large, Western-style prison island floating like a mirage.

This was the prison world constructed within Natsuki Minamiya's own dream—the Prison Barrier, used to incarcerate fiendish sorcerous criminals. Because it was Natsuki's dream world, sorcerous criminals sealed within that world had all their abilities sealed away. Even the Fourth Primogenitor, the World's Mightiest Vampire, would prove no exception.

The moment Kojou was dragged into the Prison Barrier, escape would be impossible. However, even though he knew this, Kojou could do nothing to stop it.

"Shit?! What are these chains...?"

Even his vampiric brute strength operating at full power could not even get the chains Natsuki had unleashed to flinch. Even though they were little thicker than the chain of a necklace, they had incredible strength. Furthermore, they possessed the power to seal demonic energy, leaving Kojou unable to summon his Beast Vassals.

"Senpai!"

The sight of Kojou dragged toward the gate, his resistance futile, brought a nervous look over Yukina as she shouted. However, Yukina could not move hand nor foot, either. Even if her Sword Shaman's Spirit Sight allowed her to see an instant into the future, eight submachine guns were trained upon her; it was impossible to evade them all.

And if she displayed the slightest resistance, the armed guardsmen would pull the triggers without hesitation.

Thus, Yukina could not move. If she fell there, no one would be left to liberate Kojou from the Prison Barrier. Furthermore, if Kojou's time was wasted in the Prison Barrier, Nagisa would fall into even more peril.

Sensing the magical energy of the gate as it drew nearer behind him, Kojou ground his teeth in agitation.

The next moment, he heard an odd voice full of confidence from a most unexpected direction.

"Laeding—chains forged by the gods, is it…? Quite a rare magical object you have there. That's Natsuki for you."

"What?"

Natsuki's eyes wavered, showing unease for the first time.

"Whoa?!"

The next instant, the silver chains that had bound Kojou suddenly melted like pieces of candy and flew apart.

While Kojou reeled, his balance thrown off by the recoil, a lump of liquefied metal climbed atop his shoulder. It absorbed the torn chains as it changed shape into a tiny humanoid figure.

"Transmutation…! Nina Adelard?!"

"Correct, Witch of the Void."

The self-declared Great Alchemist of Yore extended her liquid metal arms like whips, seizing hold of the armed guardsmen's firearms one after another. Even the Island Guard's cream of the crop could not respond to the incredibly unconventional attack. Their metallic components eaten away, the submachine guns crumbled in the guardsmen's hands.

Yukina, finally freed from the gun barrels trained upon her, poised her spear as she exclaimed, "Nina?! What are you doing here…?!"

"Kanon was concerned about the two of you, as it were."

Nina lifted her chin with pride. Apparently, Kojou and Yukina being in a clearly distressed state had worried Kanon, so she had covertly ordered Nina to spy on them.

"I see… So this is your doing, Astarte?" Natsuki's lips curled with displeasure as she glared at the homunculus girl.

It was Astarte who had snuck Nina in without Kojou or Yukina ever noticing. Nina had been hiding under the apron of Astarte's maid outfit.

"Do not scold her so, Witch of the Void. In spite of being a homunculus unable to defy the commands of her master, she desperately exerted herself for Kojou's sake."

Astarte stood still without a word as Nina defended her, the corners of her lips curling up with delight.

Astarte might well have known from the start that Natsuki intended to capture Kojou. However, she had been unable to convey that to Kojou and Yukina.

Hence, Astarte had assisted Nina's espionage.

As a homunculus, she could not defy Natsuki's orders. However, Natsuki had not included in her orders a clause stating *Don't bring Nina with you.*

"I heard the entire story. Would it not be better to be courteous and send Kojou and Yukina on their merry way, Witch of the Void?"

"For a pet, you certainly run your mouth…!" Natsuki spat. Being lectured so casually by Nina, her elder, was a sore spot for her.

During that time, the Island Guard personnel did not simply stand idly by and watch. Be it with shock batons or barehanded, they attacked Kojou and Yukina one after another.

"Urk!"

Yukina engaged immediately, but there were too many of them. Even Yukina, with close-combat ability capable of overwhelming demons, could not put eight armed guardsmen out of commission in a single moment.

Four guardsmen went after Yukina to slow her down while the other four went after Kojou. They, trained in anti-demonic combat, were not opponents an amateur like Kojou could take on hand to hand. *This is bad*, he thought, his face stiffening before the triumphant guardsmen. However—

"Nin!"

Suddenly, a female knight in a long-skirted garment appeared behind them. Taking the guardsmen completely by surprise, she bowled them over one after another, all in the span of an instant.

"Justina?!"

"Are you safe, Sir Kojou? By command of the Royal Sister, I, Kataya Justina, am humbly at your service!"

As Kojou stood dumbfounded, Justina knelt before him, courteously greeting him. Then she took a metal, grenade-like sphere out of her garment's sleeve. She slammed the sphere into the floor, causing pure-white smoke to spew forth.

"A magical energy diffusion screen... You little meddler."

Natsuki audibly clenched her teeth. Apparently, the smokescreen Justina spread about had the effect of inhibiting the transmission of magical energy. It only affected sorcery that manipulated things at long range, but against Natsuki, a specialist in teleportation, it was extremely effective.

"Lady Nina!"

"Mm-hmm, leave it to me."

When Justina called out to her, Nina released a dazzling beam of light from her fingertip. This was a heavy metal particle cannon—in other words, a particle beam.

The incandescent ray punched through the building's exterior wall, creating an escape route to the emergency stairs by brute force.

"Sir Kojou! With Lady Sword Shaman, while you still can!" Justina shouted while holding the rest of the Island Guard off.

"Sorry! You're a lifesaver!"

"Thank you very much!"

Thanking Justina and the others, Kojou and Yukina headed for the emergency stairs. With Natsuki unable to teleport, she had no way to pursue them.

Watching them make their escape, Justina turned to face Natsuki. Already, she had taken all the Island Guard guardsmen out of commission. However, that still left the Attack Mage. If Natsuki was serious, there was no proof Justina and Nina put together could stop her. Even with the magical energy diffusion screen interfering with spells, it was unclear how effective that would be against a witch.

However, in spite of Justina's and Nina's wariness, Natsuki showed no sign of making a move. The small-statured witch sullenly raised one cheek, sighing quietly.

"To think Nina Adelard and that cheerful foreigner would make a spectacular mess of this room so soon after the New Year..."

Natsuki glanced at the hole punched into the building's outer wall before giving the pair an exasperated look.

"Mm-hmm. Though it pains me to draw my bow upon the mistress of the household, try to overlook this, Natsuki. If you insist upon a clash of arms, I shall indulge you, but isn't your sorcery somewhat poorly matched against mine?"

Nina sat cross-legged on a fallen guardsman's back, giving Natsuki a venomous smile. However, Natsuki did not take the bait; she shooed the two off with a hand.

"No need, Nina Adelard. You having crushed the Island Guard's special forces was a great service."

Then Natsuki slowly rose to her feet. As the armed guardsmen groaned in pain, she gazed indifferently down upon them, speaking with a hint of anger.

"Tell your superiors at the Gigafloat Management Corporation…, 'I did it your way, and *this* is the result.' From here on, I shall do as I please."

The incredible sense of majesty emanating from Natsuki's entire body made the faces of the guardsmen twist in fear.

Justina and the others gazed at the unexpected spectacle, bewildered.

6

After running from Natsuki's mansion for over ten minutes, Kojou and Yukina arrived at the shopping district in front of the train station.

Since shopping malls ran New Year's bargains, there were a lot of people passing through that day. Even Natsuki was unlikely to engage in combat in such a place. With that in mind, Kojou's feet came to a halt. He'd just about hit the limit of his endurance.

"We should be fine now, right?"

"Yes, most likely. I used every incantation to obstruct pursuit that I have," Yukina replied, holding a paper scroll for *shikigami* in her hand.

Natsuki, able to employ teleportation magic, could instantly catch up to them no matter how far away they might be. However, Kojou and Yukina were probably safe so long as the trail was cold.

"This sucks, though. I didn't think Natsuki would be against it to that extent," Kojou murmured, exhausted, catching his ragged breath.

He hadn't been so naive as to think Natsuki would help them stow away without a fuss. However, being nearly stuffed into the Prison Barrier all of a sudden had never crossed his mind.

"I am also mindful of the fact she called the Island Guard straightaway."

"Well there's that, too... That's not really like her..." Kojou scowled a little as he agreed with Yukina.

Natsuki was an independent federal Attack Mage. She wasn't part of the Island Guard. Also, Natsuki had no reason to seek their assistance. By herself, she had more combat power than the Island Guard's special forces put together.

In the first place, Natsuki's teleportation magic was at its most effective when used to launch a surprise attack from anywhere, anytime. It wasn't well suited for group combat, the Island Guard's specialty. If Natsuki had been seriously trying to capture them, doing it herself would surely have been more effective.

Yet, Natsuki had made Kojou and Yukina face the Island Guard regardless. In other words, Natsuki hadn't been going all out earlier...?

Kojou shuddered when that possibility sunk in.

It had probably been a warning. She'd made them confront the Island Guard to reveal the fact that the Gigafloat Management Corporation was working to stop Kojou from leaving Itogami Island. Additionally, now that they'd broken the Island Guard's encirclement, the Gigafloat Management Corporation had only Natsuki left to rely upon. Next time, she could capture Kojou without anyone getting in her way.

What a mess, thought Kojou, unwittingly gazing up at the heavens. He'd meant to ask her to help him slip out, but as a result, he'd only created an incredibly formidable foe.

"—From the looks of it, negotiations failed, I take it?"

Kojou and Yukina walked down the sidewalk immersed in a feeling of despair when a voice suddenly called to them. The familiar voice made Kojou gasp and lift his face.

Away from the pedestrians, a black-haired girl in an old-fashioned sailor uniform stood beside a tree along the roadside.

"Kiriha Kisaki...!"

Yukina instantly went into a fighting stance as she shot Kiriha an angry look. Subconsciously, Kojou went on guard against Kiriha as well. Her waiting for them made it abundantly clear she'd watched them run from Natsuki's mansion with their tails between their legs.

"You followed us, didn't you?! For that matter, it's 'cause you went and blabbed to Natsuki that this got more complicated to begin with!"

"I merely thought it would minimize the time spent negotiating."

However, the Priestess of the Six Blades of the Bureau of Astrology spoke with a composed tone.

"I anticipated you would rely on Natsuki Minamiya from the very beginning, and I thought the chances of her assisting were fifty-fifty, so…"

"She ended up tryin' to stuff me into the Prison Barrier all of a sudden, you know?!"

Kojou's outburst at Kiriha was tinged with anger, but Kiriha's expression was oddly sober as she nodded.

"Yes. Thanks to that, I know for certain."

"You know what?!"

"That Natsuki Minamiya and the Gigafloat Management Corporation knew of the project being conducted at Kannawa Lake from the very beginning, most likely because the Lion King Agency spoke to them about it beforehand."

"What…?"

Kiriha's firm declaration rocked Kojou, making him suddenly feel lost at sea.

Yukina's expression grew tense and hard. If Kiriha's words were true, they'd given Natsuki and the Corporation the information, leaving only Yukina in the dark—regardless of her close relationship to Nagisa, the person concerned, and Kojou.

Simple abdication of responsibility could not explain such a thing. The Lion King Agency had purposefully walled her off from the information.

"Well, get going. You don't want Natsuki Minamiya to catch up to you in a place like this, do you?"

Gazing with satisfaction at Yukina's distress, Kiriha pointed to a vehicle parked at the rotary: an unobtrusive, navy-blue station wagon. Sitting in the driver's seat was a man wearing gray work clothes and a hat over his head, not standing out in any way—he was likely a Bureau of Astrology member as well.

As urged by Kiriha, Kojou and Yukina sat in the back of the station wagon. It wasn't that they trusted the Bureau of Astrology, but they judged that changing locations by car was an effective way to evade Natsuki's pursuit.

Kiriha sat in the back as well, turning to face Kojou and Yukina. Seeing this, the driver got the station wagon going.

When the station wagon left the train station rotary, Yukina glared at the girl with the traditionally-styled black hair and asked, "You said that the Gigafloat Management Corporation knew from the beginning what was happening at Kannawa Lake?"

"Yes, I did."

Kiriha, still holding her tripod case as she sat, added a smile as she replied.

"Then," said Yukina, lowering her eyes as she breathed in, "it was the Lion King Agency's plan to use Ms. Minamiya to stop senpai from leaving the island?"

"Is there any other sound explanation?" Kiriha answered, smiling in a charming yet teasing manner.

"Perhaps she knows more about this incident than we at the Bureau of Astrology do. You could try meeting Natsuki Minamiya again and ask her."

Kojou interrupted their conversation and declared, "No need for that. We'll just go and see for ourselves."

At that point, Kojou and Yukina hardly needed to ask what Natsuki and the Lion King Agency intended. Whatever the reasons, they meant to obstruct Kojou's passage to the mainland. Knowing that was plenty.

"I see. Sound reasoning."

Kiriha raised her eyebrows in an apparent show of praise. She must not have expected Kojou would recover so quickly from the shock of Natsuki's betrayal.

"But how do you intend to reach the mainland without Natsuki Minamiya's cooperation?"

"No problem. I still have one idea for getting off the island."

"The *Oceanus Grave II*—the cruise ship of Dimitrie Vattler, Duke of Ardeal, yes?"

Kiriha replied first as if she was reading Kojou's thoughts.

Taken by surprise, Kojou's mouth twisted; then he sighed and nodded.

Moored at Itogami Harbor, the giant oceanic cruiser *Oceanus Grave*

II was owned by Dimitrie Vattler, a vampire native to the Warlord's Empire. Vattler bore the title of ambassador extraordinary and plenipotentiary, so even Natsuki and the Gigafloat Management Corporation ought to be unable to touch him.

It took about half a day to travel from Itogami Island to the mainland by ferry. Of course, it wouldn't be as fast as an airplane, but he wasn't in any position to complain.

"The inside of his ship is sovereign territory, so even the Gigafloat Management Corporation can't touch us there, right? I'll get him to take us to the mainland some way or other. To be honest, it's not an option I really wanted to consider."

"That method will prove rather...costly."

"I know that, but there's no other way, so we've gotta do it!" Kojou ground his teeth in visible anguish as he lamented.

The first hurdle was whether Vattler would warmly welcome Kojou's request or not. He'd certainly run his mouth claiming to offer his love to the Fourth Primogenitor, but at heart, Vattler was a simple combat maniac, a man with few hobbies save lethal duels with powerful foes. Kojou couldn't even imagine what kind of tortuous compensation a man like that would demand in return.

If it was just picking a fight with Kojou, that'd be one thing, but worst case, the relic of The Cleansing would pique Vattler's own interest. Kojou didn't really want to think about it, but the odds of Vattler also landing on the mainland, running rampant any way he pleased, were not zero.

Perhaps Kiriha also grasped that danger, for she shook her head at his words and said, "There may well be another option."

"Huh?"

Kiriha tendered an envelope right before Kojou's and Yukina's surprised eyes. Inside the envelope were documents of various kinds with photos of Kojou's and Yukina's faces on them.

"What's this?"

"The Bureau of Astrology has arranged a private business jet. If you use a civilian corporate airstrip rather than Itogami Central Airport, the formalities to leave the island will be minimal. These are fake IDs and the necessary documentation."

"…What's your game here, Kiriha Kisaki? Why are you going this far for us…?" he pressed, more suspicious than he was gracious.

Certainly, the terms were tempting. The Bureau of Astrology was an organization with a long history. Identification cards provided by them were, in effect, as good as the real deal. If they had these, there would no longer be any need to rely on risky plans like stowing away.

Besides, if they had a civilian business jet, it would be far easier for them to move on their own. Even the Gigafloat Management Corporation could not do as it pleased with a civilian aircraft.

However, creating false identity documents and chartering a private jet were undertakings requiring considerable money and resources. Kojou couldn't come up with a reason why Kiriha and her people would sacrifice so much to get Yukina and him to the mainland.

However, Kiriha somehow seemed delighted as she turned her eyes to Kojou and said, "Would you be dissatisfied if I said 'Resentment of the Lion King Agency' and left it at that?"

"Resentment?"

"As you are aware, the Bureau of Astrology and the Lion King Agency have diverging interests. Perhaps it is as they say: *Familiarity breeds contempt*? But now, the Bureau of Astrology has good reason to confront the Lion King Agency head-on. After all, it still has its tail between its legs from the recent failure at Blue Elysium."

"…What does that have to do with giving me a hand?"

Kojou knit his brows, bewildered by Kiriha's lack of a direct reply.

Kiriha sarcastically narrowed her eyes and said, "The Lion King Agency is exceptionally afraid of you paying a visit to Kannawa Lake. How can we not make use of that? It is akin to tossing dirty laundry into the house of a neighbor you do not care for."

"So you're treating me like dirty laundry…?!" Kojou growled.

Kiriha giggled and broke into a smile. "Surely, Fourth Primogenitor, it is not a poor arrangement for you. Our interests coincide in this matter. Though, I'm sure she has conflicted feelings as a member of the Lion King Agency."

Kiriha shook her head a little in a show of pity and shifted her gaze to Yukina.

"Yukina Himeragi. If you wish it, I do not mind if you bow out here and now. I will take over the duty of watching the Fourth Primogenitor."

"That will not be necessary."

Yukina easily let the cold, sharp words of the Priestess of the Six Blades wash over her. *Oh my*, Kiriha seemed to say, with Kojou sensing surprise from her at how Yukina did not hesitate for even a moment.

"Whatever the Lion King Agency has in mind, there has been no change in my assigned mission. Watching the Fourth Primogenitor is my duty."

"I see… But should you not ask if this is what the Fourth Primogenitor wishes?

"What senpai wishes…?"

"Perhaps this is a harsh way to put it, but am I, with the full support of the Bureau of Astrology, not more useful to him than you, abandoned by the Lion King Agency? Rescuing Nagisa Akatsuki is his top priority, after all?"

"Er…" Yukina bit her lip, unable to refute her.

Setting aside that it was uncertain whether Yukina had been abandoned per se, the fact remained that the Lion King Agency had withheld a great deal of information from her. Of course, Yukina had neither chartered a jet nor arranged false identification for him.

"Surely you understand who is more suitable to watch over you, Fourth Primogenitor?"

"Uh, this isn't really about being more suitable or not…" Kojou, suddenly confronted with the matter, seemed conflicted as he looked from one to the other.

While Kojou did so, Kiriha gazed at him with upturned eyes and smiled seductively.

"I forgot to mention this, but appearances notwithstanding, I am actually an F cup."

"—What? Seriously?!"

Without thinking, Kojou fixed his gaze upon the cleavage of Kiriha's sailor uniform. Kiriha's physique was slender, so she really didn't feel like someone with gravure idol-level breast size.

"Senpai…!"

As Kojou marveled, wondering if her clothes made her chest look smaller than it really was, Yukina shot him a contemptuous glare. Then Kiriha giggled and smiled in visible delight.

"I lied."

"You were lying?!"

Kojou wailed, feeling exceptionally wounded. For some reason, Yukina was covering her own breasts with a hand as she breathed a sigh of relief. Kiriha made another teasing smile.

"I am sorry to get your hopes up, but my breasts are rather disappointing."

"Er, it's not that my hopes were raised, but anyway, I don't need a babysitter. I can't trust you very much, for one thing. Besides, this isn't because Himeragi's my watcher. She's cooperating with me 'cause she's worried about Nagisa."

"I see… If that is what you believe, do as you like."

Kiriha gazed with amusement as Yukina's expression changed in the face of Kojou's words.

"And for the record, if you had a jet ready to go, you should've mentioned that at the start, sheesh. Then we wouldn't have Natsuki attacking us like that—"

"In that case, would the two of you have believed what I had to say?" Kiriha's smile oozed with malice while she pressed the matter further. "You are relying on the Bureau of Astrology because Natsuki Minamiya has turned against you. Am I mistaken?"

"You might be right…but that's because—"

"Yes, a natural judgment. I can understand that much." Kiriha shrugged as if the matter didn't concern her.

The Bureau of Astrology she belonged to had attempted to use the living weapon known as Leviathan to sink Itogami Island not even a month before. That had resulted in the Bureau of Astrology's plans ending in failure, but that fact didn't make Kojou trust Kiriha and her people 100 percent, either.

This time, Natsuki turning against them had backed them into a corner, forcing them to accept Kiriha's cooperation. Kiriha surely understood that fact for herself. She was not particularly trying to scold them for it.

"Incidentally, these ID cards… They, uh, list Himeragi and me as husband and wife…?"

Kojou was checking the contents of the envelope handed to him when he posed the question to Kiriha.

According to the forged documents, Kojou was an eighteen-year-old employee at an electrical installation company, and Yukina was his twenty-nine-year-old wife. Granted, Yukina had something of an adult air about her, but he wondered if having her pose as someone pushing thirty was a bit excessive. Somehow, he suspected the age notation was Kiriha's malice showing through.

"Being treated as an adult is convenient when concealing one's identity, is it not?"

"Well, you might have a point, but…did you need to make us husband and wife?"

"I was unable to acquire any other suitable fake IDs. You will have to use them to the best of your ability."

Kiriha had said as much without a hint of ill will, but Kojou still uttered an "Ugh…" and fell into silence. This, too, was no doubt her resentment expressed in a roundabout way, but even so, her Bureau of Astrology was the only thing he could rely on at the moment.

Yukina unexpectedly refrained from speaking a single dissatisfied word—gazing at the ID card treating her as Kojou's spouse, she didn't seem all that put off by it.

"So where is this business jet your people arranged?"

Kojou turned his eyes toward the window of the moving station wagon as he asked.

"Island North's industrial airport."

"There, huh…?" Kojou grimaced.

The industrial airport in Island North was one of Itogami Island's five civilian airstrips. Kojou had used it once before, but he didn't have very good memories of it. At the time, the aircraft he flew on wound up stranding him on a deserted island in the middle of the ocean.

Thus, Kojou wasn't particularly surprised when he saw Yukina's face abruptly freeze over.

He was sure it was the fear of that time coming back to her, but—

"Stop! Stop the car, quickly—"

Yukina leaned forward and shouted at the driver, but the eerie presence made Kiriha react immediately as well. The two were staring at the space above the road—a straight coastal road with little in the way of traffic.

"Huh?!"

The driver was perplexed. He did as he was told, stepping on the brakes and pulling the station wagon toward the road's shoulder. His hand was reaching for the hazard light—all natural actions for him to take.

A moment later, slender silver chains were spat out from thin air, forming a giant net before them. The navy-blue station wagon was unable to reduce its speed enough to avoid plunging straight into the net and being ensnared within.

"A-aaaagh?!"

The front window finely cracked. The driver let out a cry as he became buried in a deployed airbag.

But Kiriha was in motion before that.

With a single palm strike, she pounded down the station wagon's hatch behind Kojou and the others with incredible force. The hatch blew off, giving Kojou and the rest an open path to the rear.

"Th-the hell?!"

Kojou, frozen in shock, had Yukina firmly gripping his right arm and Kiriha firmly gripping his left. The two dragged Kojou with them as they leaped out of the still-moving vehicle.

Considering their antagonistic relationship, it was unthinkably splendid teamwork. Even if Kiriha was part of a different organization—a Priestess of the Six Blades, also known as the Black Sword Shaman—Yukina and Kiriha employed the very same martial art.

"Uooooooo?!"

In contrast to the steady landings of Yukina and Kiriha, Kojou's momentum from jumping out of the car sent him rolling on the ground back first. But had they not leaped, Kojou and the others would already have found themselves pulled into the net of silver chains, wagon and all.

"I told you I could not let you go, Kojou Akatsuki."

Kojou and the others trembled when they heard a powerful voice above them.

As the station wagon was suspended in thin air, a woman with a parasol and an extravagant dress landed on its roof without a sound. She,

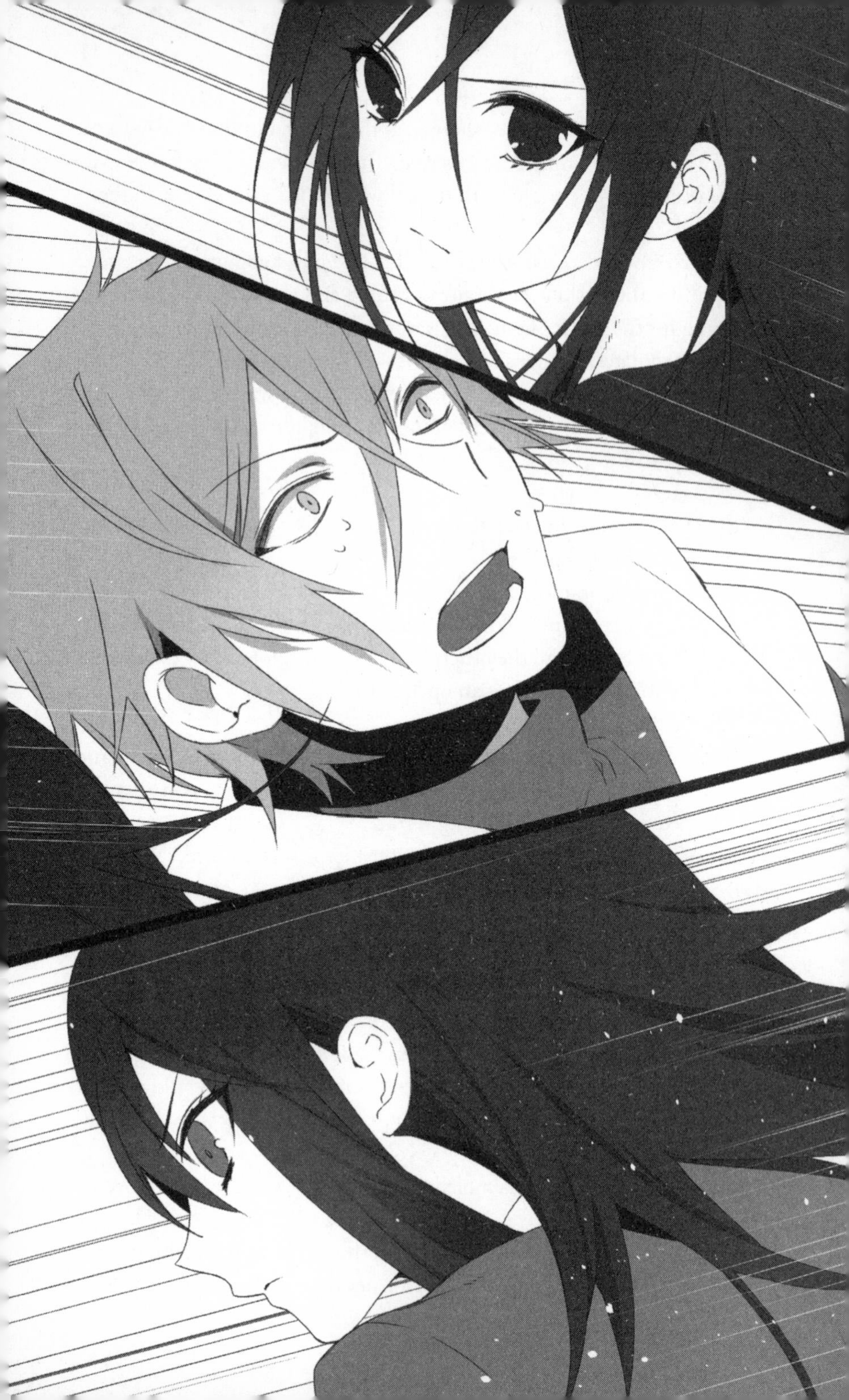

blessed with a beautiful face reminiscent of a doll, gazed emotionlessly down at Kojou and the others.

"Natsuki...!"

Dumbfounded and groaning in pain, Kojou uttered the name of the witch shrouded in black magical energy.

However, Natsuki no longer had words to spare.

Instead of warnings, she shot out a barrage of silver chains, raining down like countless spears.

CHAPTER FOUR
THE WITCH OF THE VOID

1

Silver sparks buried the midday sky.

A high-pitched roar reminiscent of a scream made Kojou's eardrums tremble. Metal clashed against metal, creating a ragged sound that resembled the atmosphere of the battlefield itself.

With Snowdrift Wolf, Yukina knocked down the countless chains Natsuki loosed from the void.

"Leap, Fourth Primogenitor!"

"Wh-whoa!!"

Yukina alone could not fend off all of Natsuki's attacks—Kiriha judged as much in an instant, pushing Kojou's back and sending him flying. Kojou sailed over the edge of the concrete curb and slid down to the sandy beach below.

Leaping after Kojou, Kiriha drew her own spear from her tripod case. The shaft slid and lengthened, its twin prongs entwined in a spiral until they spun and deployed, becoming like the tines of a tuning fork. With her gray, forked spear thus emerged, Kiriha struck back against new chains aimed at Kojou.

Natsuki employed a teleportation spell to appear in front of Kojou and Kiriha. Yukina leaped after her, landing on the sandy beach. The three on Kojou's side faced off against Natsuki atop white resin-made sand spread over an artificial coast.

"I see... You did not allow Kojou Akatsuki to escape. You waited for him to move to a place away from prying eyes. Is that not so, Witch of the Void?"

Forked spear poised, Kiriha gazed at Natsuki with a sullen look. She'd gone as far as arranging a getaway car to cover their tracks, but in the end, she had only played into Natsuki's hands. From Kiriha's point of view, that had to be a significant dent to her pride.

"Correct, little girl. If that idiot ran riot inside the city, it would be more trouble after the fact."

Natsuki replied in an apathetic voice. She seemed to barely acknowledge Kiriha's existence. This got on the Black Sword Shaman's nerves even more.

"Ugh," Yukina groaned, gripping her spear with added strength, but even she did nothing reckless like attempting to cut Natsuki down. Of course, Yukina knew full well that Natsuki's words were only taunts.

"You said you couldn't let me leave Itogami Island, didn't you...?"

Instead, it was Kojou who murmured to her in a low voice.

Kojou clenched a fist as faint rage coursed through his entire body. Naturally, her chasing him this far meant Kojou had no choice but to harden his resolve as well. If Natsuki seriously meant to stop him, Kojou had to fight her, too.

"Is that why, Natsuki?! You wanna fight me, for *that*?!"

"Do not address your teacher by her first name, fool."

Natsuki dipped the tip of her still-folded fan in Kojou's direction. That instant, an incredible impact assailed Kojou's forehead. The Fourth Primogenitor, feeling fierce pain as if he'd been struck with an iron maul, staggered and fell to one knee.

Yukina and Kiriha, standing at Kojou's flanks, gasped, astonished. Even they, completely on guard, had been utterly unable to respond to Natsuki's attack.

"Ugh...!"

"I did not come here to play fight you. Unlike that Master of Serpents, troublesome things like this are not a hobby of mine, and I do not do them because I like to. If you go into the Prison Barrier like a good boy, I won't have to hurt you."

Natsuki, continuing to elegantly hold her parasol, spat her words like venom.

Kojou gritted his teeth as he lifted his face. "There's no way…I can do that…!"

"If you will be lonely by yourself, I can send that transfer student to accompany you…or perhaps you would prefer Aiba?"

"I'm not talking about that!" Kojou wobbled to his feet as he howled raggedly at Natsuki. "I'm gonna save Nagisa. After that, extra lessons or Prison Barrier—I'll do whatever you want. So please let me go for now! Or are you gonna go bring back Nagisa in my place?!"

"Bring back Nagisa Akatsuki…?" Natsuki let out a small sigh as she shot Kojou a stark look. "Do you seriously believe you can do that?"

"What?!"

"Ahh, no. Not in that sense. Of course, Nagisa should be coming home safe and sound—so long as you do nothing rash."

Natsuki shook her head a little at the sight of Kojou consumed by a primal rage. Then she lowered her eyes in a show of pity and said, "It is you, specifically, who cannot bring her back, Kojou Akatsuki."

"…What do you mean by that?"

"If that which is at the bottom of Kannawa Lake is what the Lion King Agency expects, you cannot come into contact with it and escape unscathed."

Her reluctant tone shook Kojou faintly. He sensed seriousness from Natsuki's explanation that went beyond a simple attempt to intimidate.

"And what makes you say that?"

"That's how these relics of The Cleansing are. You have experienced this for yourself, have you not?" Natsuki smiled sadly.

What is she talking about? thought a perplexed Kojou when countless, fragmented images crammed into the back of his brain without warning. A rock-strewn, sun-swept land. A coffin of ice. Within it, a girl with hair spanning all the colors of the rainbow. Then, the scent of blood—

"G…uoa…?!"

"Senpai?!"

When Kojou moaned, stricken by a powerful headache, Yukina instantly put an arm around him to support him.

Kiriha appeared perplexed. She did not know that Kojou's memories had been consumed or that fragments of those memories were causing Kojou this pain.

"It seems the conversation has come to an end," Natsuki cruelly murmured as she looked down at the anguished Kojou.

One way or another, he no longer possessed the strength to resist her. It took all his mental strength to remain conscious in the face of the torrent of onrushing memories.

"We will speak more of this inside the Prison Barrier…provided you truly wish to know, that is."

Natsuki quietly raised her left hand. A ripple-like distortion occurred in the air above her head, with silver chains unleashed from within.

"Don't mess…with me…dammit…!"

Kojou glared at Natsuki as the chains entwined around his right arm. With all his vampiric muscular strength, he somehow shook off the chains trying to drag him into the midair distortion.

"If the existence of the Fourth Primogenitor's connected to The Cleansing, what the hell is the Lion King Agency involving Nagisa for?! She's not connected to any of it!!"

"Not connected…? Do you truly believe that?" Natsuki smiled scornfully at Kojou's rebuttal, speaking the words in a tone rich with implication.

Kojou did not understand the meaning of her words.

Nagisa was not a vampire. She'd already lost her spiritual powers. So, of course, the Fourth Primogenitor and The Cleansing had nothing to do with her. She couldn't be connected.

"…?!"

But Natsuki's question clearly unnerved Yukina. The expression Kojou saw on her face was one of naked fear.

"It would seem this strikes a chord with you, transfer student," Natsuki commented calmly. She would not let Yukina's consternation slip by.

Yukina continued gripping her silver spear, nodding affirmatively without a word. "You don't mean…Avrora…?"

Her terrified reaction forced Kojou to realize the truth.

Avrora Florestina, the twelfth Kaleid Blood—Kojou had inherited the power of the Fourth Primogenitor from her. Moreover, Avrora was no more. To save Nagisa from the wicked soul called Root Avrora, she had sacrificed herself, perishing in the process.

But what if Avrora's soul remained, even to that day?

It was not impossible—if a powerful enough spirit medium kept her soul connected to the world. No, it was not out of the question for someone with abnormally high spirit-medium power, such as Nagisa Akatsuki once possessed—

"Avrora's still inside Nagisa?! They're trying to use Avrora to check out that relic of The Cleansing thing?!" Kojou, completely recovered from his confusion, shouted in raw anger.

It wasn't that he'd subconsciously known all along; it simply made too much sense. It provided a reason for Nagisa, a powerful spirit medium, to have lost her spiritual abilities. It explained why she had deteriorated without an identifiable cause. If that was the cost of keeping Avrora's soul connected to the world of the living, it answered a number of Kojou's unanswered questions.

Nagisa probably wasn't using her abilities on purpose. However, if the result was to give Avrora's soul peace, Kojou could hardly blame his little sister. If anything, it made him proud of her.

I won't forgive anyone for using Nagisa and Avrora's soul for their own convenience, thought Kojou. Not even if it was the work of the Lion King Agency.

Natsuki bore the brunt of Kojou's anger head-on, stating in a matter-of-fact tone, "I shall set your mind at ease about just one thing. The Lion King Agency has no intention of putting Nagisa Akatsuki in peril. It is the reverse. For the sake of their objective, they shall surely protect your little sister, even unto death."

"Yeah…? Hearing that puts me at ease."

Kojou stripped off the parka he wore as he unwittingly cracked a small smile.

"You're cooperating with the Lion King Agency 'cause you know they're not trying to put Nagisa in danger, right, Natsuki?"

"Of course. Your sister or not, she is one of my pupils all the same."

Natsuki replied without hesitation. Kojou, expecting that reply, nodded with satisfaction.

"Himeragi…that means the Lion King Agency didn't betray you, right?"

"Ah…!"

Yukina looked at Kojou, large eyes opened wide. Kiriha snorted, unamused.

To Yukina, caught between her loyalty to the Lion King Agency and her friendship with Nagisa, Natsuki's words were salvation. The Lion King Agency wasn't trying to use Nagisa as some sort of sacrifice. Knowing this, Yukina could trust in the Lion King Agency. Half the reason for her anguish had vanished.

"Thanks to that, I'll keep on respecting you, Natsuki. Even after I beat the crap out of you, so you'll let me go to— No, I'm going to the mainland, no matter what it takes!"

Dense demonic energy coursed out of every pore of Kojou's body like lava from a volcano.

"If the Fourth Primogenitor's power is needed to get some relic of The Cleansing thingy, that's not Avrora's job. It's mine. Whatever reason people have, I'll crush anyone using Nagisa and Avrora for their own convenience! From here on, this is *my* fight!"

"Hmph…"

As Kojou came rushing in with a demonic energy-infused fist, Natsuki held him in check with a single lash of her fan.

New chains unleashed by Natsuki assaulted Kojou from four directions. Kojou unleashed his demonic energy like an explosion, shooting them down one after the next. However, Natsuki's attacks did not relent. Then, when an attack came from Kojou's blind side that he didn't think he could dodge, a silver spear lashed out, knocking it down with a ferocious shower of sparks.

"No, senpai. This is *our* fight—!"

Yukina, wearing a dazzling smile free from worry, landed at Kojou's side.

"—Himeragi?!"

"I now understand very well why the Lion King Agency left me at your side, senpai."

As Yukina stared at Natsuki, her eyes held the powerful glint of restored confidence.

"To stop senpai from running amok, he requires a watcher who will act in concert with him until the very end, no matter where he might go—even if, as a result, the Lion King Agency itself stands in the way. That is why they did not inform me, so that senpai would not see me as his enemy—"

"That is quite a self-serving interpretation, but certainly, it is far from impossible. Unlike a relic of The Cleansing that may or may not even exist, the Fourth Primogenitor is a clear and present danger. He cannot be left to his own devices."

A faint, pained smile came over Natsuki's lips.

Though not the Agency's unanimous opinion, Yukina had been left as Kojou's watcher. She had not been abandoned; it was the opposite. Yukina had been isolated from all information to keep their trump card, the one-and-only World's Mightiest Vampire, in a controllable state.

"And now that you know this, what of it? Will you become my enemy, Sword Shaman of the Lion King Agency?"

Natsuki's tiny body floated softly in defiance of gravity. The space around her distorted irregularly, much like flames. Magical energy, so vast that it rivaled Kojou at his most serious, circulated around Natsuki's flesh.

"Move aside, Natsuki! Even you can't take Himeragi and me when we're serious!"

"Quite an interesting thing you've just said, student of mine."

Whoosh! went Natsuki's left arm, lashing out.

Immediately, Yukina, purportedly gripping her spear, was sent flying back, unable to even raise her voice. With a ferocious sand cloud rising, she slammed into the beach some four to five meters behind him.

"Himeragi?!"

Kojou stared, scarcely believing his eyes as Yukina went down without breaking her fall. He had never seen her get taken down in such a one-sided way before. Neither her Spirit Sight nor Snowdrift Wolf's ability to nullify magical energy had been able to block Natsuki's attack.

"Gah?!"

The instant Natsuki's gaze shifted toward him, Kojou's vision went blurry. There was neither pain nor impact, but Kojou lost his equilibrium, almost like he was intoxicated.

Kojou instinctively realized teleportation magic had been used to directly shake his brain. Vampiric healing ability was of no use unless it was an actual physical injury.

Feeling his mind grow distant, inching past the point where he could resist, Kojou desperately held on to his senses.

"You think the two of you can defeat me? You shouldn't underestimate your elders."

With his vision in pieces, like he was looking through a kaleidoscope, Kojou saw Natsuki looking down at him with scorn.

Then, with a twirl of her parasol, Natsuki unleashed countless chains toward the immobile Kojou.

2

"You, the girl over there, halt! Halt!!"

The men, clad in black body armor, ran down the connecting walkway inside the airport.

Asagi listened to their footsteps behind her as she dashed down the stairs. The men were part of the Island Guard airport security unit and, on top of that, an Attack Squad armed with anti-demon firearms.

Of course, there was no reason for such men to be targeting Asagi, yet they were, in fact, chasing her nonetheless.

"If you do not obey this warning, we will use force in accordance with Demon Sanctuary law!"

"Huh?!"

Asagi looked back without thinking when glass shattered above her head. It was a simple warning shot, albeit extremely accurate.

"Wait a— Mogwai, what's going on?! They're seriously shooting at me!" Asagi shouted at her AI partner as she desperately avoided the glass shards raining down.

"Keh-keh." Mogwai laughed, his demeanor clearly amused. *"They're adhesive polymer rounds for capturing demons. Glue rounds, in other words."*

"Capturing?! They cracked glass just now like it was nothing, you know?!"

"Well, I suppose getting pumped with glue rounds still hurts a lot."

"What the hell?! Why are they coming at me with stuff like that?!"

"The bottom line is: Someone doesn't want you to leave Itogami Island, li'l miss," Mogwai responded calmly to Asagi's worked-up shouting.

Asagi had ended up being chased by the Island Guard just before embarking on an airplane headed for the mainland. It was plain that no one had been after Asagi prior to that point; after all, Mogwai had his paws on every surveillance camera on Itogami Island, so no one could have been using them to tail her.

"So they're involved in that whole Nagisa thing?!"

Asagi's breath was ragged as she ran down a freight hoistway alongside the parking lot. It was supposed to be off-limits, but fortunately, there was no sign of an airport employee to scold her. The Island Guard people seemed to have driven them off beforehand.

"Left at the next corner, li'l miss."

Mogwai was reading the guardsmen's movements and giving instructions accordingly. Asagi, no longer aware of even her own current location, shut up and did as he told her. But—

"—Wait, this is a dead end?!" Asagi exclaimed as she was suddenly driven into a cul-de-sac.

A despairingly high steel fence blocked her path. The fence had several layers of barbed wire laid on top, so climbing seemed out of the question.

When Asagi nervously looked back, Island Guard guardsmen had already surrounded her. Asagi stood in place, shocked as their glossy-black gun barrels were trained on her as one.

"Nah, I've got it handled. I thought this might happen, so I called a bodyguard over, you see."

Asagi's surprised ears heard Mogwai's voice—a voice seemingly proud of victory.

"Bodyguard…?"

Just when that word left Asagi feeling conflicted, there was a dull, explosive roar behind her. The impact was reminiscent of a direct hit from a missile; she was sent flying. She hit the ground and collapsed.

A section of the concrete foundation smashed apart, rending the iron fence to pieces. Rolling over the wreckage, a spectacularly gleaming crimson weapon of land warfare emerged. It was an anti-demon, four-legged, micro-robotic tank designed for urban environments that seemed almost like a living creature. Its targeting camera whirled around to look at Asagi.

Without a moment's delay, the armed Island Guard guardsmen attempted to engage, but antipersonnel submachine guns had no hope of penetrating tank armor. In contrast, the robot tank opened fire with antipersonnel machine guns embedded in its front legs, mowing the guardsmen down. Even if they were nonlethal rubber bullets, the might of the 7.62 mm machine guns was tremendous, nonetheless. The guardsmen cried out as they were sent flying—antiballistic vests and all.

"Seems that I made it in time, Empress."

"You're...Tanker?!"

Asagi's mouth dropped open as she heard the voice flowing out of the tank's external speakers. The voice with a lisp; the anachronistic, over-the-top verbiage—she knew only one person with those defining features.

"Indeed, I am. I, Lydianne Didier, hath arrived in accordance with Sir Mogwai's request," replied Lydianne Didier, Asagi's peer from her part-time job and a rare hacking genius in her own right, in a round-about, grandiose manner.

"...Hey, what do you think you're up to?! This is totally an act of terrorism, isn't it?!"

Asagi nervously pressed the point as she surveyed the flattened armed guardsmen.

It seemed that the tank-riding girl was the bodyguard Mogwai had arranged. For whatever reason, Lydianne had some kind of crush on Asagi, so she was no doubt happy to be called upon...and this tragic spectacle was the result. When added to blowing away the iron fence with the tank's main gun, no matter how you sliced it, this was well beyond the realm of protecting.

However, Lydianne let out a cheerful laugh and said:

"'Tis not a problem. If we make a clean getaway, they shall cover it up after the fact. They have no more interest in this going public than thee."

"Well, you might be right about that, but...!"

"More importantly, Empress, gaze upon parking spot 404 on the south side."

"Eh?"

Using a manipulator for hands-on work nestled in the tank's torso, she deftly pointed to a parking lot flanking a runway. Sitting there was the Pandion—a tilt-rotor, multi-role transport plane made by Didier Heavy Industries.

"I humbly took the liberty of putting that transport on standby. With it, thou may flee to the mainland. 'Tis best to run in this case."

"Well, I suppose I do have to get on an airplane here…"

Asagi slumped her shoulders as she accepted the inevitable. It wasn't like she could just go back to the airport terminal and board her passenger plane like nothing had happened.

That said, staying on Itogami Island presented its own dangers. Even if the Island Guard concealed what had happened like Lydianne had said, that required things cooling down.

"Indeed, 'tis so. Now then, quickly, straddle me."

"Straddle…er, where?"

Asagi looked back with concern as the robot tank minimally lowered itself. The robot tank was heavily curved to defeat incoming rounds; it had no obvious place for a human to ride.

However, without hesitation or warning, Lydianne used the manipulator arm to pick up Asagi.

"Hey, you…! Wait a… E-every-everyone can see!"

The robot tank rushed to the parking lot, heedless of Asagi's efforts to hold down her skirt.

However, the robot tank did not go even ten meters before it stopped with a *clunk*. The joints of the four limbs supporting the tank's body lost their tensile strength; the armor scattered sparks as it crashed against the ground.

"Nn?! Gah…?!"

"What now?!"

Sounds of frustration over losing control of her tank trickled out from Lydianne's lips. When Asagi looked harder, she saw glowing symbols of light emerging from the ground at the tank's feet. The semi-corporeal familiars these summoned were clinging to the tank's joints.

"Gremlins. Island Guard Attack Mages."

Mogwai calmly analyzed the situation.

Gremlins were a special kind of spirit for military use that excelled at making machines and electronic devices go on the fritz. They were of little value for attacking fellow Attack Mages, but against modern weaponry, like a robotic tank, they were tremendously effective.

"What the hell are they sending Attack Mages after a high school girl with a legit part-time job for?!"

"Setting virtue or legitimacy aside, using magic against a tank seems to have been a good call."

Mogwai replied casually, like it was no problem of his. The fact was that making its electronic devices run amok had put Lydianne's tank out of action. However heavy its weapons, a robot tank that couldn't move was no different than a paperweight.

"Mogwai, can't you do something?!"

"No can do. Thanks to the gremlins, there are malfunctions in electronic devices all over the area. To be honest, just maintaining this connection is getting...tou...gh..."

"M... Mogwai?!"

The AI's sarcastic voice had a frail, broken ring to it. The gremlins were affecting even Asagi's smartphone.

Cut off from digital networks, Asagi was rendered nothing more than a powerless high school girl.

During the time Asagi was unable to move, Island Guard reinforcements arrived, and Asagi found gun barrels trained on her once more.

"This is bad...!"

Asagi unwittingly closed her eyes in the face of desperate peril. The very next moment, Lydianne's tank suddenly restarted. With a heavy *whirlll*, the tank turned, protecting Asagi from the armed guardsmen's gunfire; in contrast, the machine-gun rounds unleashed by the tank mercilessly gunned down the careless guardsmen.

"—Tanker?!"

"I am sorry to have caused you concern. 'Tis disgraceful."

She heard Lydianne's bashful voice over the speakers once more. At some point, Mogwai's signal had come back, too. The gremlins had vanished without a trace.

"How did you break the spell...?"

"'Twas not I. Rather, it was—"

As Lydianne spoke, her targeting camera moved. Asagi turned her head the same way.

A man in a black Chinese garment was standing atop the grass of a taxiway. He was a bespectacled young man with delicate features. His right hand was holding a long, strange-looking spear with tips on both ends.

And someone from the Island Guard was lying faceup at his feet—the Attack Mage controlling the gremlins.

"You're...the fugitive who was at MAR!" Asagi shouted, tensing up.

The man in the black clothes resembled some kind of ancient mystic. Asagi had met this man once before.

The young man had casually appeared, seemingly to test Asagi's abilities firsthand. He departed after overwhelming Yukina with his combat capabilities.

"I am. Please forgive my reluctant and prolonged silence, Priestess of Cain." The youth in black clothes put a hand to his chest and politely bowed toward her.

"What did you...do to that person...?!"

"You need not be concerned. The recoil from the spell being broken merely rendered the individual unconscious. There is no value in shedding the blood of such a lowly caster where thy eyes may see."

"So you came to save us, then...?"

Asagi looked wary as she glared at the youth holding the spear in his hand. She'd heard that the black spear he called Fangzahn could annihilate magical and spiritual energy in the area around it.

The youth in the black outfit had used that spear's power to defeat the Island Guard Attack Mage.

"I only did what was expected. After all, thy wish is also the wish of my King." The youth shot Asagi an adoring gaze as he spoke in a gentle tone.

Asagi felt a shudder through her entire body and stated with annoyance, "What the hell...? You can't just leave that hanging out there...!"

"*He* is waiting for you. All is according to the will of our King—"

The youth in black lowered his head with reverence and backed away, clearing the path for Asagi.

"*There's no time, li'l miss. Island Guard reinforcements will arrive within five minutes.*"

"*Empress!*"

"I get it. Let's go, Tanker."

Spurred by Mogwai and Lydianne, Asagi sighed and issued her instructions.

The tilt-rotor transport Lydianne had arranged was already prepared for liftoff. Once she and Asagi reached it, they'd be able to fly to the mainland almost immediately.

The youth in the black outfit smiled with satisfaction as he watched Asagi and Lydianne go.

"Someday, we shall meet again. Until then, have a pleasant journey."

3

The damage from distorting Kojou's brain had robbed his body of its freedom of movement. He was essentially punch-drunk. Though he saw the silver chains sailing toward him, Kojou could not move a single step.

"Sh...it... C'mon over, Natra—!!"

Kojou instantly summoned a Beast Vassal. Natra Cinereus—the Fourth Primogenitor's fourth Beast Vassal—symbolized the vampiric ability of transformation into mist. However, the ability's effective range was not limited to just Kojou; at minimum, solid matter would lose its cohesive power for tens of meters in a radius around him, transforming it all into silver mist. The fact that there was no guarantee it would return to its original form intact made Natra an extremely troublesome Beast Vassal.

Even so, that destructive power was all he could rely on to fend off Natsuki's silver chains—

"Too late."

However, Natsuki's silver chains caught hold of Kojou before his Beast Vassal could materialize. Laeding, the name granted to that relic of the Devas, sealed Kojou's demonic energy, obstructing the summoning of his Beast Vassal.

"Natsuki... Stop this...!"

"It is not *Natsuki* to you."

Visibly sour, Natsuki waved her fan with her left hand. Kojou's chain-bound body was being dragged into the teleportation gate floating in midair with overwhelming force. The gate no doubt led straight to the Prison Barrier.

Kojou no longer had the power to shake off Natsuki's chains. Furthermore, Yukina was still lying on the sandy beach.

The tension of the silver chains stretching from thin air increased, and Kojou's body was sure to be swallowed by the spatial distortion. The instant Kojou grasped this and began struggling in desperation...

Ting—went the high-pitched sound as Natsuki's silver chains were severed entirely.

"Dwaa?!"

Kojou, suddenly freed from the chains, hit the sand headfirst with great force. As he did, a black-haired girl wearing an old-fashioned sailor uniform landed beside him with a small flutter.

"If even two on one is insufficient, how about three on one?"

Whoosh! Kiriha's forked spear cut through the air, leaving a sound behind as she turned to face Natsuki.

Kojou stared up at her in surprise. If her own words were to be believed, Kiriha's objective was to spite the Lion King Agency. There should have been no reason for her to expose herself to the danger of fighting Natsuki.

Naturally, Natsuki seemed to harbor the same question as Kojou. She knitted her brows, glaring at the Black Sword Shaman with a sour look as she said, "Kiriha Kisaki...Priestess of the Six Blades of the Bureau of Astrology. What do you think you are doing?"

Natsuki unleashed an attack before she heard a reply.

The Witch of the Void assaulted Kiriha with the same invisible blast of wind that had sent Yukina flying. She created an explosive shock wave by vibrating space itself. Even if it was produced via a spell, the shock wave alone was a simple physical phenomenon, which was why Snowdrift Wolf's magic-nullifying ability could not defend against it. Of course, it was impossible for a slender spear to parry a shock wave of pure force.

However, without a word, Kiriha lashed out with her forked spear. The next moment, with a great roar, the invisible shock wave barreling toward Kiriha dissipated.

Kiriha had blocked the shock wave with a physical wall invisible to the naked eye.

"How unfortunate, Witch of the Void. I had hoped to establish a favorable rapport between us, but…"

Kiriha spoke in a frigid tone as she waved away the rising cloud of sandy dust.

"Pseudo-spatial severing. I thought that trick belonged to the Lion King Agency's ponytail girl?"

"It appears I was correct to copy that abominable Shamanic War Dancer's ritual just in case…"

"I see… The Bureau of Astrology's Ricercare… A rather convenient toy."

Natsuki voiced her words of praise in a largely disinterested tone.

The ability of Kiriha's forked spear was an emulation of ritual spells used by others. To the Priestesses of the Six Blades, experts in anti-demonic beast combat, switching among several abilities according to the circumstance was far more advantageous than a single, powerful ability.

Kiriha was using this ability to re-create the ritual used by Sayaka's Lustrous Scale, employing an enchantment to copy the effect from severing space itself—thus, a pseudo-spatial severing ritual.

The crack in space created by these attacks obstructed any physical attack. It was this slice in space that had fended off Natsuki's shock wave.

"But being a copy, it has surely inherited the weaknesses of the original."

The shock wave could not defeat Kiriha. Having made that judgment, Natsuki reacted quickly.

Like an extraordinarily skilled juggler, Natsuki scattered about tiny creatures from inside the parasol she held. At first glance, they resembled teddy bears. It was a horde of adorable, two-headed beasts.

With agile motions belying their appearance, the beasts surrounded Kojou and Kiriha.

"What the heck are those things…?!"

Kojou could not hide his bewilderment at being surrounded by the cluster of cute critters. *Maybe their adorable appearance is supposed to rob us of our will to fight*, wondered Kojou in the back of his mind.

However, Kiriha glared hatefully at the beasts and said:

"Witch's familiars. If you let them touch you, they'll send one or two of your legs flying."

"...Are you serious?!"

"...The pseudo-spatial severing cannot defend against an attack from all directions at once."

"Don't tell me that was her plan...?!"

Kiriha's calm murmur made Kojou's face go cold.

Lustrous Scale's seemingly invulnerable bulwark had a number of weaknesses. One was that the crack in space only faced a single direction. A second was that the effect only lasted for an instant. If Natsuki's familiars rushed them all at once, Kiriha could not fend them off alone.

"Fourth Primogenitor!"

"I know! C'mon over, Al-Meissa Mercury—!"

The horde of beasts leaped at them from all sides. Kojou summoned his Beast Vassal before even seeing the creatures. The vast demonic energy he scattered about solidified into a quicksilver-scaled, two-headed dragon, the Dimension Eater. With its enormous maws, the two-headed dragon swallowed Natsuki's familiars—and the very space they occupied—whole.

"—Reverberate!"

Kiriha launched an attack through the crack between the overwhelmingly destructive attacks. She fished out thin metal sheets from the cleavage of her uniform, and these transformed into a pair of black leopards.

Simultaneously, Kiriha herself leaped into action, spear in hand.

Thanks to Kojou's Beast Vassal's rough eating habits, the space around them was torn asunder. Even Natsuki could not teleport under those circumstances. She'd no doubt judged this was the time to strike Natsuki down.

And Natsuki made no move to elude the attack. Rather than evade it, she opted to counterattack.

Wind coiled around her with a heavy roar as new chains shot out. However, the thickness of these chains was far greater than Laeding. These were steel anchor cables tens of centimeters in diameter thick. Each and every single link of the chain was now its own, vile weapon. Dromi, launched with all the force of a cannon, became a giant cudgel that came swinging at Kiriha's familiars from the side.

The black leopard *shikigami* were smashed into pieces with ease.

"Oh n—!"

Using her forked spear as a shield, Kiriha barely managed to fend off a square hit by the chain. However, she could do nothing about the shock wave created by the chain's sheer mass.

"Kiriha?!"

When Kiriha was blown away, Kojou tried to rush over to her, but Natsuki's Dromi—the accursed chains—assaulted him. Kojou just barely managed to evade them, and though his balance was heavily thrown off, he subconsciously threw up both his arms, half out of instinct and half out of fear.

As Kojou did so, his face was struck by an invisible shock wave. The Dromi attack had been a simple decoy. Natsuki's real attack was the blow from his blind spot a moment later.

"Hmph… It would seem you have learned a little."

Natsuki spoke in apparent praise as her chains returned to the unknown void from whence they came.

"I'm against…corporal punishment…dammit!" Kojou wheezed raggedly as he glared at Natsuki.

His having blocked her shock wave was mostly the product of coincidence. If he hadn't guarded his chin, this vibration to his brain would have surely finished him. But even if he hardened his defenses, he couldn't picture that helping take her down. There was no way forward except engaging in a reckless attack.

"Come to think of it…your body that's here is a clone made with magic, isn't it?"

Kojou put his breath in order as he posed the question. Natsuki was not a simple sorceress, but a witch. A witch's ability to freely manipulate a vast quantity of magical energy was granted to her via a pact with a devil. And that pact came with a cost. Natsuki was no exception to that rule.

The cost imposed on Natsuki was "sleep."

As the warden of the Prison Barrier, she had to continue to sleep—and dream—for all eternity. She was never to grow old, never to touch the flesh of others, simply to continue to dream—

The Natsuki standing before Kojou and the others was a doll she had made using magical energy. In other words, it was nothing more than part of her dream.

"And what of it?"

Natsuki calmly inquired as if to say *Why bring that up now?*

Certainly, the Natsuki there was a clone. That was also why she was invincible. Even if they defeated her clone, they could not inflict a single scratch on Natsuki's real body. Even Aya Tokoyogi, a fellow witch, had needed to create a massive upheaval involving all of Itogami Island and pry open the Prison Barrier to attack Natsuki's real body.

Of course, Kojou could do no such thing. Nor did he *need* to.

The gist was that all he needed to do was destroy Natsuki's clone and temporarily render her powerless. During that time, Kojou and the others would reach the airport and get off the island.

"I just wanted to know for sure. In other words, there's no point holding back, is there?"

"That is tantamount to claiming you could beat me if you didn't hold back."

Natsuki spoke with an exasperated tone. The majesty surrounding her threatened to crush Kojou flat, but—

"Sorry, but I have a lot riding on this, too!"

Kojou swept aside that fear and summoned a new Beast Vassal. This was a solemn, ferocious beast over ten meters long, a lightning lion scattering electric flashes everywhere.

The chains Natsuki wielded were convenient from Kojou's perspective. Electricity would pass through the chains to Natsuki. Even if Natsuki engaged in attack, the lightning lion could use those chains to transfer damage to her.

However, Natsuki's expression did not change. She gazed down at Kojou's Beast Vassal, turning to her own shadow and issuing a single, solemn command.

"—Awaken, Rheingold."

That instant, a giant emerged behind Natsuki that towered over even Kojou's summoned beast.

It was a humanoid figure clad in golden armor, rich in both elegance and savagery—a golden, clockwork knight.

Its malevolent presence made the very man-made ground shake.

From inside the thick armor, seemingly locking darkness itself within, Kojou could hear the rumblings of giant gears and motors that sounded like a monstrous roar.

"What the hell is that…?!"

Kojou subconsciously backed up a step as he looked up at the giant knight.

It was not that the quantity of magical energy overwhelmed him. Certainly, the golden knight was emitting incredible magical energy, but the same went for Kojou's Beast Vassal. The nature of their power was simply…different.

The golden knight construct gave off an air that was clearly not of that world. It was black, devilish power that consumed light.

"Don't tell me…this is your Guardian, Natsuki?!"

Kojou finally arrived at the golden knight construct's true nature.

A Guardian was a devil's vassal granted to a witch as compensation for the pact with the devil. As the word suggested, the Guardian protected the witch and granted her the power to fulfill her wish. And should the witch abrogate that pact, it became the executioner that would reap the witch's life—

In other words, a so-called Guardian was the physical manifestation of the pact with a devil. Accordingly, its strength was proportional to the weight of the contract. Considering the cost Natsuki had paid, Kojou imagined that her Guardian must be mighty indeed.

Even so, the malevolence of the golden knight construct was twisted far beyond Kojou's expectations.

And yet, that didn't change what Kojou had to do.

"Regulus Aurum—!"

The giant lightning lion turned into a thunderbolt that slammed into the golden knight construct from the front.

An incredible explosion erupted, and a supersonic shock wave parted the sea. The fifth Beast Vassal of the Fourth Primogenitor, Regulus Aurum, had once scorched an entire Gigafloat district in an instant. That power remained undiminished.

In the sky, black clouds began to gather, drawn in by the lightning lion's energy. The ferocious aftershocks shook the entire island. The electromagnetic waves made digital devices go crazy, and the area around the coast had surely suffered considerable damage.

However, Natsuki's Guardian did not fall. Enveloped in dazzling brilliance, it was the lightning lion that roared in anguish.

Crimson thorns unleashed by the golden knight construct had entwined around the lightning lion, pinning it in place.

Kiriha, watching how the battle proceeded with an astounded look, murmured, "It is holding back a Beast Vassal of the Fourth Primogenitor… through brute force…?!"

Put more accurately, the golden knight construct was not pushing the lightning lion back. It used the crimson thorns like a net, preventing the lion from moving. But it had withstood the attack of the Fourth Primogenitor's Beast Vassal all the same.

"G…uoooooooooo?!"

"Futile, Akatsuki… Gleipnir cannot be torn apart."

Natsuki solemnly smiled at Kojou as he desperately tried to control the lightning lion. And this time, the silver chains she unleashed caught Kojou completely.

"Fourth Primogenitor!"

Yukina, collapsed on the sandy beach, had no power left with which to rescue Kojou.

Kojou's body was swallowed up by the spatial distortion, sinking into the watery void, and vanished.

"Senpai!" Yukina, finally regaining consciousness, screamed in a forlorn voice.

4

Blast winds swirled around with a great roar.

The guardrail and lampposts running alongside the coast were mowed down, and the sandy beach was heavily gouged out.

Two bearers of enormous magical energy had clashed—the Fourth Primogenitor's Beast Vassal and Natsuki's Guardian. Surely, it was fortunate that so *little* damage had been done.

"So this is the Witch of the Void's Guardian…Rheingold, that which plunged the demons of Europe to the depths of terror. It would seem the rumors are true… It warps this world's time and space merely by its presence."

Kiriha sullenly swept her sand-smeared black hair as she groggily rose to her feet. Then, she made a weary sigh as she returned her forked spear to its carrying form.

When Natsuki saw Kiriha abandon her combat posture, she seemed disappointed as she inquired, "Already finished, Priestess of the Six Blades?"

The Beast Vassal of the Fourth Primogenitor was still materialized. However, its power seemed insufficient to break through the net of thorns, perhaps due to the loss of Kojou, its host. Restrained by the golden knight construct that was Natsuki's Guardian, all it could do was continue its ragged snarls.

Seeing this for herself, Kiriha unenthusiastically shook her head and said, "Now that the Fourth Primogenitor is held captive in the Prison Barrier, further combat is fruitless, is it not?"

"A wise decision."

Natsuki narrowed her eyes as she spoke. In spite of the combat that had just taken place, Natsuki wasn't even winded. She was displaying a margin for error seemingly without limit.

Even if Kiriha continued the fight alone, there was surely little she could do. The difference in power was simply too great. In any case, her opponent was a monster who'd overwhelmed the World's Mightiest Vampire.

"However, it would seem that is not what the girl over there thinks," Kiriha murmured with apparent delight as she shot a sidelong glance behind her.

Yukina, presumed flattened by Natsuki's attack, was rising to her feet, using her spear to support her weight.

Even at that moment, Yukina's legs trembled from her wounds. Despite that, the will to fight against Natsuki had not faded from her eyes.

"So another recalcitrant pupil remains…" Natsuki sighed slightly. Then she turned to face Yukina and said, "It is as you see, transfer student. Your target for observation has been captured. Yet you still intend to fight?"

"I believe I stated it at the beginning. This is my fight as well." Yukina quietly readied her spear.

Snowdrift Wolf, able to nullify magical energy and rend any magical barrier, was the mortal foe of witches like Natsuki. In terms of pure combat ability, Natsuki was overwhelmingly superior, but if Snowdrift Wolf's edge even grazed her, their positions would be immediately reversed.

Of course, Natsuki was no doubt well aware of this. She coldly looked back at the wobbly Yukina, and slowly raised her left hand. She gave the fan she held within it a small flutter.

The air screeched, violently being torn asunder as Natsuki launched chains out of thin air.

However, Yukina knocked all the chains down with a bare minimum of movement. Her reaction speed suggested she knew the course along which each of the countless chains would fly.

"The Spirit Sight of a Sword Shaman of the Lion King Agency… Divining the future, then? I see. You are well trained."

For once, Natsuki praised Yukina.

Meanwhile, Yukina sprinted toward her. Pure-white sand swirled up as she approached within her spear's reach in one go. With a light *tap*, Natsuki kicked off from the ground and danced in midair. Yukina leaped in pursuit.

Then, a charming smile came over Natsuki as the air warped before her eyes—a shock wave cannon produced via spatial control.

"But you rely on your Spirit Sight too much… Hence why you fell for such a simple trick."

"Ugh…!"

Natsuki's lecturing words made Yukina's expression harden. Even her Spirit Sight could not see the invisible shock wave. Even if she knew in advance the shock wave was coming, she didn't know when—or what course it would take.

In any case, it was impossible for Yukina to evade a launched shock wave while in the midst of her leap.

Therefore—the only way left for her was to slice her way through.

"Snowdrift Wolf!"

Yukina poured all the spiritual energy she had into the silver spear. The enchantment inscribed upon Snowdrift Wolf activated, causing it to radiate a pure-white light. This was the light of the Divine Oscillation Effect that nullified magical energy.

"So you blocked the spatial control spell creating the shock wave with a Divine Oscillation Effect barrier…"

Realizing that her attack had misfired, Natsuki instantly retreated.

"—I, Maiden of the Lion, Sword Shaman of the High God, beseech thee."

Yukina landed with her spear at the ready. She pursued Natsuki once more as her lips wove a solemn incantation.

Amplified by Yukina's spiritual energy, the Divine Oscillation Effect grew more radiant still. The light collected at Snowdrift Wolf's spear tip, forming a single, giant blade.

It was a radiant blade of light reaching several times her height.

"O purifying light, O divine wolf of the snowdrift, by your steel divine will, strike down the devils before me!"

Yukina swung the blade horizontally, finally catching Natsuki's body. It grazed Natsuki's slender torso, gouging a deep wound that reached nearly to her spine.

However, the lack of feedback from the blow caused Yukina to gasp in shock. Natsuki's body, which should have been nearly cleaved into two, vanished without a trace.

"An illusion—?!"

"Did I not tell you? You rely too much on your Spirit Sight."

Natsuki's statement came from behind the confused Yukina—her disappointment apparent.

Silver chains shot out from thin air. Having focused all her spiritual strength into her attack, Yukina had no strength left with which to fend off the chains. The chains wrapped around her four limbs, rendering her unable to move or act.

"How immature. Relying on a toy like this while losing sight of what is important."

Natsuki spoke in a pitying tone as she opened the gate once more.

She meant to bring Yukina to the Prison Barrier, too. Once dragged into Natsuki's dream, it would be impossible for her to escape on her own power, even with the capabilities of Snowdrift Wolf.

Yukina desperately struggled, but the chains mercilessly pulled her body toward the gate.

"It's over," the Attack Mage said dismissively.

"No, not yet."

A moment later, a girl in an old-fashioned sailor uniform swung down a gray blade from Natsuki's defenseless back.

Natsuki easily evaded the attack, but she had not been Kiriha's target. Her pseudo-spatial severing blade rent apart the silver chains binding Yukina's limbs.

"What are you playing at, Kiriha Kisaki?"

Natsuki folded her fan and shifted a sour look toward Kiriha. Yukina, freed from the silver chains' bondage, also looked up at Kiriha in surprise.

"I changed my mind. I'm *so* sorry."

However, Kiriha's pleasant smile contained not even a hint of shame. She twirled her forked spear around, turning the twin tips toward Natsuki. The gesture was a clear declaration of war.

"Even if she is an apprentice, seeing a Sword Shaman from the Lion King Agency proper so easily defeated makes me, a Priestess of the Six Blades, sometimes referred to as a Black Sword Shaman, sick to my stomach. I shall thus render a touch of aid."

It was unclear just how much of Kiriha's declaration was how she really felt.

Natsuki replied with apathy, "Do as you like. The result will be no different."

"I wonder about that. You're awfully stuck-up for a mere witch. Perhaps death will humble you."

Speaking those words in a belligerent tone, her true nature bared, Kiriha glanced over to Yukina.

Yukina nodded without a word, readying her spear at Kiriha's side.

Natsuki gazed tediously at the light and dark Sword Shamans, supposed enemies now fighting side by side, and sighed.

5

When Kojou came to, he was standing in a Spartan room featuring stonework.

The walls were built with uneven, natural stones, and there was a small, iron-barred window. It was what you'd expect from an antique prison straight out of the Middle Ages.

"Here again…"

Kojou squatted down and looked up at the ceiling. The sunrays shining in from the window were the color of blood. He faintly remembered the scenery. Kojou had been in this room once before. The fact that his memories of it were uncertain was likely because this was inside the world of dreams.

This was the Prison Barrier, the world Natsuki had constructed out of her own dream.

The walls appeared rugged and thick, but not so thick that a Beast Vassal of the Fourth Primogenitor could not break them.

Kojou tried to call a Beast Vassal over, but the results were as he expected. He felt no sign of a Beast Vassal appearing. For that matter, he could no longer sense his own demonic energy.

"Give it up. You cannot employ your Beast Vassals within this space. It is my dream, after all."

As Kojou continued his futile efforts, someone spoke to him from behind.

At some point, a luxurious reclining armchair had appeared in the center of the room. Seated upon it was an adult woman wearing a white shirt and a tight miniskirt.

She was about 165 centimeters tall; she was probably about twenty-six years old.

She had the delicate beauty of a doll, but her vainglorious eyes, seemingly looking down on all before her, made that impression go to waste. The woman, characterized by long, black hair, was holding an elaborate lace fan.

"And you look like that because it's a dream, too?"

Kojou sighed deeply, as if wholly exasperated by the sight. "Hmm-hmm," went the woman in the tight miniskirt, smiling proudly as she said, "I matched appearance with my actual age."

"Well, you certainly do come off pretty grown-up with that look…"

Kojou voiced his half-baked appraisal.

Her appearance might have changed, but the woman's tone and personality were all Natsuki. Thanks to that, he didn't feel put off very much. If anything really stood out, it was the extremely large difference

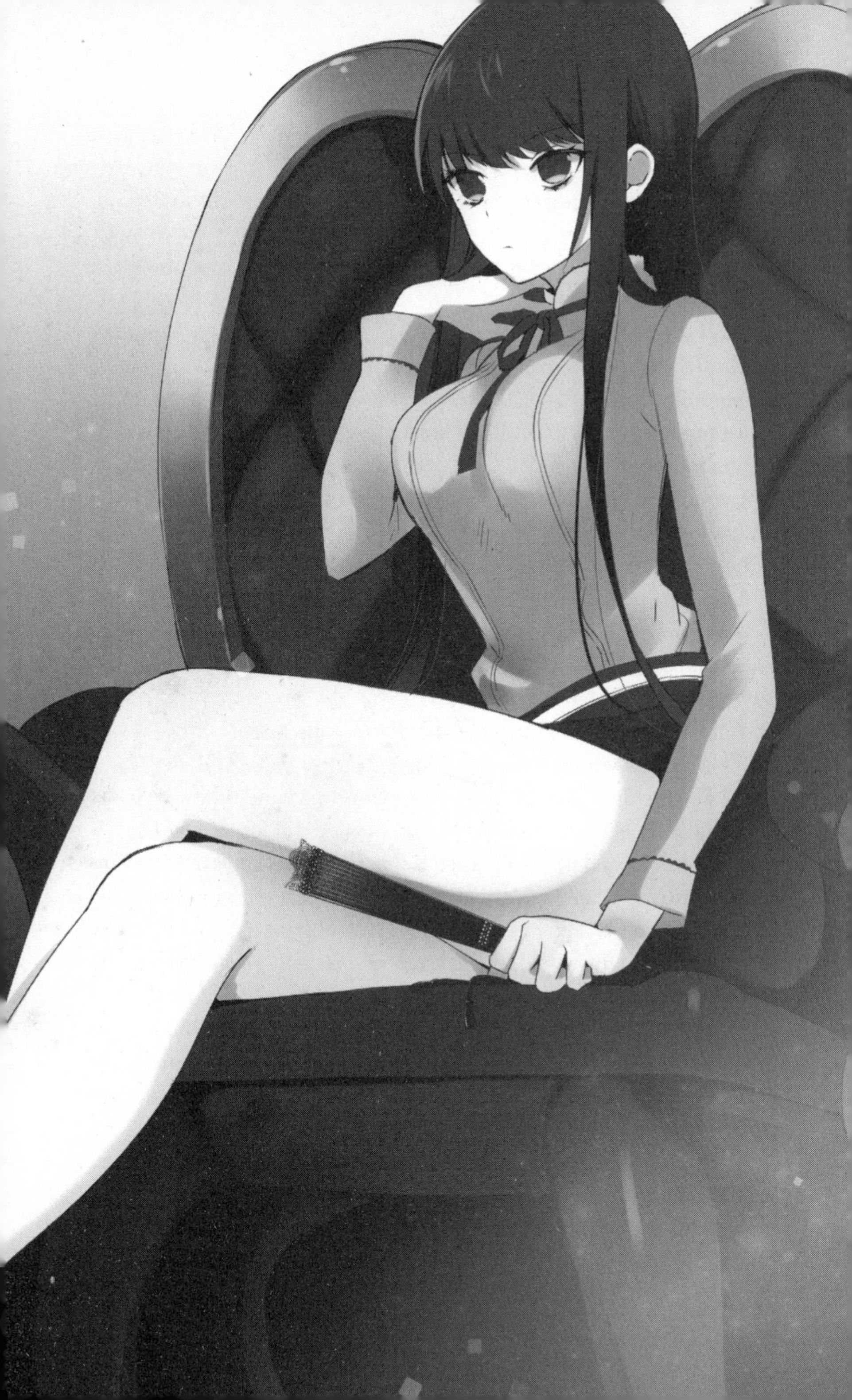

in bust size, but pointing *that* out would only anger her, so he kept his mouth shut. This was Natsuki's dream world after all.

"Your face says you have not yet given up on going to the mainland, Kojou Akatsuki."

Adult Natsuki recrossed her legs, highlighted by her pumps and black tights.

Kojou kept sitting cross-legged on the floor, nodding like a sulking child as he said, "Of course not. I still haven't heard from you why you're trying to stop me."

"An explanation, is it? Would you be dissatisfied to hear that I do not wish to lose you?"

Natsuki's expression was oddly serious as she made the statement. That really threw Kojou off.

"Lose...? You mean, dying? I am a vampire, you know..."

"A vampire primogenitor cursed with immortality by God...yes?" Her tone was most unamused. "Hmph. And if, on the mainland, you met a being who could slay that very God? Could you really speak of your own immortality so casually then?"

"Kill God... You're tellin' some tall tales at your age..."

Kojou turned toward Natsuki, who was giving him a look that was a little like pity. Sure, Kojou's title of the World's Mightiest Vampire was far-flung in itself, but he thought Natsuki's words far too great a leap.

However, Natsuki calmly ignored Kojou's rudeness and said, "By God I mean in the sense of the creators of the system we know as the world...a God at least on the level of the ancestor of all humankind."

"Ancestor of humankind... The first human, then? That sounds pretty mythological, but..."

"I suppose so. One can view the mythos from every corner of the globe in various ways... He did as the God that created him commanded, or perhaps, he slew that God, and the children of this later God became the rulers of a new world?"

"So that's what you mean," said Kojou, accepting Natsuki's words.

Like vampiric primogenitors, the *original* human brought to life by a mythical Creator was said to be unaging, undying, remaining himself in myths the world over.

"But in the end, which side is this founding god the founder of?" Natsuki muttered the words, almost like she was asking herself that question.

"What do you mean, which?"

"Isn't it obvious? Humans or demons?"

Natsuki seemed bored as she pressed her chin against her hand.

"This is not a matter of which is superior, but humankind and demonkind differ immensely. Though they speak the same languages, and it is even possible for them to crossbreed, they differ too much as living beings. Is it not unnatural to think of the two as descendants of the same gods?"

Kojou began to sense an ill premonition as Natsuki readily continued.

Why did the race known as demons exist in the world...? Scientists and theologians the world over continued to pose that question, and to that day, no final answer had been found. It was said that Demon Sanctuaries existed to unravel that very mystery.

"And if, say, the ancestors of humans and demons turned out to be brothers, would there be a problem with that?"

Kojou aired a rather naive question. After all, if the two had been created by the same God, the two ancestors were equals. The descendants—humans and demons—had no supremacy over the other. Neither race was evil. And yet—

"It is the other way around," Natsuki answered, smiling with scorn. "There will be conflicts so long as different peoples exist. It goes the same for the gods."

"So a war among the ancestors, huh?"

"It is something that happened long enough ago to make the mind grow numb. No proper records of it remain."

"Oh... Okay...," Kojou murmured at Natsuki's words.

Just because two sides were equal didn't mean they would get along. If anything, it was *because* they were equal that enmity between them deepened. Now that she mentioned it, such things were all too typical, and the same apparently went for these ancestors.

"So in the end, what happened to them? The battle's over, right?"

"Who knows? Even I do not know the truth about The Cleansing in any detail. Perhaps they destroyed each other, were both sealed away, or even slain by weapons built to slay the gods."

"...Weapons?"

The disturbing echo of that word made Kojou's look turn grave. Natsuki gazed at his expression, cruelly curling up the corners of her lips as she said:

"Within the memory of Avrora Florestina, the Fourth Primogenitor was called a god-killing weapon, yes? The gods were warring against one another. Is it strange that weapons for slaying gods would be constructed? And the Fourth Primogenitor is not necessarily the only god-killing weapon that still exists."

"......"

Kojou's silence was like a lament.

He was remembering Leviathan, which he had previously encountered at Blue Elysium. According to scripture, it was the Serpent of Jealousy, the mightiest of all creatures fashioned by the gods. The demon beast was off the charts, several kilometers in length, and was called a living weapon from the age of myth and legend.

What if, like that monster and the Fourth Primogenitor, other god-killing weapons had been built and still existed?

And so—

"You're saying the relic of The Cleansing at the bottom of Kannawa Lake is one of those god-killing weapons?"

"We do not yet know. Nor, for that matter, which side it belongs to."

"Which side...?"

"There are two types of relics of the so-called Cleansing. In other words, there are weapons to kill the ancestors of demons, and weapons to kill the ancestors of humankind."

"...!"

Natsuki's nonchalant explanation sent a cold shudder up Kojou's spine.

"Both would be dangerous beings, but if they obtain a weapon for annihilating the ancestors of humankind, less so... Far less than the alternative," she continued.

Kojou could only grimace in silence.

Since the dawn of recorded history, humankind and demonkind had waged incessant conflict against the other, and only in recent history had they achieved something resembling peaceful coexistence. Thanks to the Holy Ground Treaty, formed some several decades prior, peace had finally become a reality.

This had come about because of the efforts of the First Primogenitor, the Lost Warlord, and because humanity was tired from a long war. However, the more practical reason why the treaty had been signed was that the science and magic humans possessed had evolved to the point of rivaling the military might of demons. In short, there was a concern that human and demon civilizations would both collapse.

And what would happen if either camp obtained a weapon powerful enough to throw the balance of power askew? There was no point imagining—the result was all too clear.

"I get why the thing at the bottom of Kannawa Lake is dangerous," Kojou said after a long sigh. "But what does that have to do with Nagisa and Avrora?"

"…The Lion King Agency is not considering digging up the relic of The Cleansing," Natsuki replied, shrugging. "Their objective is to neutralize it—to seal away the relic about to awaken at the bottom of Kannawa Lake—this time forever."

"Seal? Wait—about to awak— Er… What the hell?! That's news to me!!"

In his surprise, Kojou pressed closer to Natsuki. Finding his approach annoying, Natsuki brushed Kojou aside with her left hand.

"Do you understand at least a little why I cannot let you go to Kannawa Lake?"

"Because you don't know whether the relic will respond to my demonic energy and just wake up faster."

"Correct."

"……"

Kojou bit his lip and grunted quietly. "Ugh."

However, he felt everything making sense deep inside of him. The Lion King Agency was a government organization. They acted with the objective of preventing large-scale sorcerous disasters and sorcerous terrorism, or so he had been told.

If an incident like that was happening at Kannawa Lake, on one level, their actions were entirely rational. He also thought that Gajou trying to take Nagisa there indicated a gross inability to read the mood.

"But isn't it just as dangerous to bring Avrora close to it?"

"It might well be."

Surprisingly, Natsuki did not refute Kojou's misgivings.

"However, even the Lion King Agency cannot use a ritual to seal a god-killing weapon of ill-known provenance. Hence, why they set their eyes on Nagisa Akatsuki."

"What for?!"

"Avrora Florestina knows a ritual to seal a god-killing weapon."

Natsuki's unexpected answer struck Kojou completely out of the blue.

Properly speaking, Avrora, one of the twelve Kaleid Blood vampires, was not the Fourth Primogenitor. She was a vessel built to contain the accursed soul of the Fourth Primogenitor—Root Avrora—that made it a god-killing weapon.

As a result of Kojou's actions and those of Avrora's herself, the soul of Root was annihilated, and she had been liberated from her duty as a sealing vessel.

However, that did not mean Avrora had lost her functionality as that sealing vessel.

"They want to use the ritual for sealing Root on the relic at Kannawa Lake? They can do that…?"

"Certainly, it is a poor gamble. But if it succeeds, no human lives will be lost. Furthermore, the Avrora Florestina possessing Nagisa Akatsuki is a psychic remnant unable to take physical form. Her effects on the relic are likely to be minimal."

"And what happens if they fail?"

When Kojou suppressed his emotions and posed the question, Natsuki displayed a sarcastic smile.

"Let's see… Best case, they might be able to tame it, much as you did with Avrora Florestina."

"And worst case?"

"That goes without saying—war."

"Wha…?!"

Natsuki's reply was exceedingly simple; moreover, it was oddly persuasive.

Natsuki and the Lion King Agency had fully anticipated the worst case long before, hence why they had made their move.

"The negotiation condition presented by Hisano Akatsuki was to free Nagisa Akatsuki of Avrora Florestina. The Lion King Agency likely has some sort of plan to save your little sister."

"Hisano… You're sayin' Grandma's the one pullin' the strings?!"

Astounded, Kojou widened his eyes. But when he thought about it calmly, it immediately made perfect sense. In spite of Gajou's wariness about being tailed, the Lion King Agency learned Nagisa's movements for one simple reason: Hisano had leaked the information to them from the inside.

"Surely, it is not so surprising. In the first place, was Gajou Akatsuki not taking Natsuki there so she could be examined?"

"Shit…! But if they save Nagisa, what happens to Avrora's soul?" he asked, clenching his fist once more.

Natsuki calmly shook her head. "There is nothing to be done. That girl no longer exists. That which is chipping your little sister's life away is nothing but a psychic remnant. It is a fragment of a soul that is already lost."

"…Why didn't you talk to me about this in the first place?!"

When Kojou glared at Natsuki in rebuke, Natsuki's expression turned haughty.

"Relax. This is my dream world. I will make you forget about all this before you leave this place, like a dream you cannot remember after awakening."

"Don't give me that crap…! There's no way I can back down after hearing all that!"

Giving into his emotions, Kojou tried to grab Natsuki by her shirt. However, his hand was repelled by Natsuki's barrier before he could touch her. Groaning from the pain, like from an electric jolt, Kojou brought his face closer to Natsuki's again.

"And besides, if you end up fighting this relic, aren't you gonna need my power?!"

"Do not get a thick head, brat. What can a shrimp unable to lay a finger on me do against a god-killing weapon?"

Natsuki's beautiful lips curled upward. This time, Kojou was sent flying, making an unsightly crash against the wall.

With his powers currently stripped from him while inside the barrier, Kojou was unable to defy her. And yet, Kojou did not relent, raising his face with a ferocious smile.

"Ain't it a little too soon to say I can't lay a finger on you?"

"Oh really...? Would you like to try escaping the Prison Barrier right now, then?"

Kojou replied to Natsuki's taunts with a nod. "If we get out of here on our own power, you'll let us go to the mainland, got it?"

"*Our power...?* Interesting. We shall see."

6

"Black Thunder—!"

With an earsplitting cry, Yukina leaped with agility that surpassed human limits. She worked her way through countless Natsuki afterimages, lashing out with spear blows resembling rays of light.

"Hmph, a physical enchantment. Certainly, you are fast, but—"

The small-statured witch easily deflected Yukina's blow, using the momentary opening to brush the girl aside with her left hand. Yukina was unable to evade the shock wave thus released, interrupting her string of attacks.

"The way you fight is too honest, transfer student. It is easy to discern your target."

"Gah...!"

With Yukina's mobility reduced, Natsuki sent her teddy bear-like familiars barreling toward her. The familiars self-destructed faster than Yukina could mount a counterattack. Yukina, sent flying by the explosive pressure, was heavily off-balance when silver chain spears shot out of thin air poured down on her.

It was a Priestess of the Six Blades in an old-fashioned sailor uniform who rescued Yukina in her moment of peril.

"Mist Leopard—Twin Moons!"

She knocked Natsuki's silver chains down using her forked spear in a slicing attack. The resulting cracks in space also fended off the blast waves from the familiars.

"Kiriha...!"

"I am sorry, but that was my last pseudo-spatial severing. Ricercare's ritual energy depletion rate far exceeds the original's."

Kiriha's statement was blunt while she lowered her forked spear—its glow now lost. The pseudo-spatial severing ability, able to sever Laeding and block the invisible shock wave, was an exceedingly effective weapon against Natsuki. Now that it had been lost, they could not help but be at a disadvantage.

"No, you have done enough."

However, Yukina stood up with a charming, forceful smile.

Kiriha looked back at her in surprise and said, "But we will be whittled down at this rate. The Witch of the Void has a wealth of composure like an instructor's."

"I wonder... Does she really?"

Yukina spoke with an oddly reserved tone. Kiriha looked at her suspiciously; Yukina behaved like she did not think her words were mere trash talk.

"If Ms. Minamiya is merely preventing senpai from escaping Itogami Island, the fact that he is locked in the Prison Barrier means her objective has already been achieved. She has no reason to fight us."

"...Certainly, you might have a point. If she teleported to Keystone Gate, there would be nothing we could do."

"Yes. Yet, in point of fact, Ms. Minamiya remains here. I believe she has a reason why she is unable to teleport at this time."

"...?!" Kiriha's lips trembled slightly.

It was Natsuki's illusion that had made Yukina realize it. This was Natsuki, someone who teleported with the same ease of breathing. There was no need for her to rely on an illusion to evade Yukina's attack; she needed only teleport somewhere beyond the reach of Yukina's spear.

However, Natsuki had used the illusion. Moreover, she was avoiding the use of teleportation, even to the point of fruitlessly dragging out the battle. Even if Natsuki could still teleport but had merely deemed it best not to, it must have had some external cause.

"You believe she acts like an instructor training us to conceal a tangible weakness?" concluded Kiriha, her lips forming a broad smile. Her face broadcast great happiness at the prospect that Natsuki's composure was hollow. She nodded. "I see, a Beast Vassal of the Fourth Primogenitor...!"

"Yes."

Yukina glared up at the small-statured witch hovering in midair. Behind Natsuki, above the ocean, was the lightning lion, trapped by a net of thorns.

"That the Beast Vassal has not dematerialized means that senpai has not given up on breaking out of the Prison Barrier, doesn't it? And to continue to keep senpai's Beast Vassal bound, you are unable to use teleportation. Am I wrong?"

"Hmph... Akatsuki being such a sore loser certainly was unexpected. For some reason, the idiot actually believes you will rescue him."

Natsuki affirmed Yukina's words with surprising frankness. *Knowing this does not change my absolute superiority in any way,* spoke her demeanor.

"In other words, Yukina Himeragi, if I capture you and drag you into the Prison Barrier, that idiot will finally give up."

Yukina listened to Natsuki's nonchalant words with a powerful glint resting in her eyes.

"Unfortunately, I believe that to be beyond your means."

"Just so you know, even if I can't teleport, I'm *very* strong—"

Before her words even reached Yukina, Natsuki gave Dromi physical form.

This steel-colored anchor chain had a diameter of ten centimeters and was hundreds of meters long. It was impossible to tell by sight how many hundreds of tons it weighed. Natsuki waved the extraordinarily huge anchor chain like a whip, sweeping it at Yukina and Kiriha.

"Tch!"

It was Kiriha who struck back against it. With her blade, purportedly unable to use pseudo-spatial severing, she severed the flying chain at its base, proceeding on with a leap toward Natsuki.

"So you did have strength left, Priestess of the Six Blades."

Natsuki lifted her chin in delight. Kiriha thrust her spear toward the defenseless Natsuki. It was at a lethal distance where even an illusion would be insufficient to escape. But:

"How unfortunate, Kiriha Kisaki."

"Oh n—?!"

Kiriha exclaimed as she noticed the silver chain wrapped around her ankle.

Natsuki had strewn silver chains under the sand around herself beforehand—a trap Kiriha had leaped right into.

Kiriha abandoned her attack on Natsuki and severed the silver chain around her ankle. Had her decision come a single moment later, Kiriha would have most surely been struck with an additional blow by Natsuki.

During that time, Natsuki escaped beyond Kiriha's range. And this time, Kiriha had truly hit the bottom of the ritual energy stored in Ricercare. That surprise attack had been her last chance to defeat Natsuki.

"That is enough to break even my heart… The difference in combat experience is too great…" Kiriha dropped to one knee on the sand and spat the words. She felt like that single instant had shaved several years off her life span.

With Kiriha like that, Yukina reluctantly spoke to her from behind. "I am sorry, Kiriha. Could you buy me just ten seconds?"

"Excuse me?!" Kiriha's eyes flew wide at Yukina's incomprehensibly selfish request. "Are you trying to be funny?! Ten seconds against that witch is putting my life on the line, you know?!"

"I know. But please."

When Kiriha vented her naked irritation, Yukina looked straight back at her as she spoke. Faced with Yukina's obstinate demeanor, the poison seemed to drain from Kiriha as she sighed deeply and said:

"Your personality is…far beyond my expectations. I sympathize with the Fourth Primogenitor somewhat."

Kiriha tossed out that sarcasm-laden line, stubbornly rising to her feet. Then Kiriha tossed away her gray forked spear. Either way, with its ritual energy spent, Ricercare was useless against Natsuki. Even knowing this, it was a highly resolute decision.

The decisiveness of the Priestess of the Six Blades brought a wary look over Natsuki's face. Kiriha, seeing this, smiled broadly as she said, "My shadow is mist, yet not mist. Blade, yet not blade."

With that quiet chant, Kiriha's entire body melted into the scenery around her, vanishing from sight. Using an illusion spell, she had manipulated the refractive properties of the air, rendering her own body transparent. Simultaneously, she had activated a concealment spell, blocking all trace of her aura.

"May it cut like a dream and sound the song of disaster—"

When her incantation was complete, Kiriha had completely vanished from sight. Even Yukina's Spirit Sight could not detect her presence. It was a frighteningly complete level of ritualistic camouflage.

"Hiding yourself to restrict my movements— Not bad."

Natsuki murmured words of praise as she summoned a horde of familiars once more. She no doubt intended to use the beasts' senses, far surpassing those of human beings, to locate Kiriha.

"Too late—!"

However, Kiriha appeared right before Natsuki's eyes before the familiars could materialize.

Heedless of the familiars surrounding her, Kiriha thrust her weaponless left hand toward Natsuki and commanded, "Fiery Lightning—!"

Then she slammed condensed, high-density ritual energy into Natsuki like a transparent hammer.

Kiriha's point-blank attack sent the familiars flying as well. Knocked away, the familiars exploded with tremendous roars, sending Yukina's black hair flapping in the blast winds.

"I see. Employing ritual camouflage for a surprise attack to buy time—"

Natsuki had only needed to retreat a little to evade being caught in the familiars' explosions. Kiriha, buffeted by the blast winds, was in no position to give pursuit.

Even so, Kiriha smirked.

As Natsuki retreated slightly, a dazzling ritual symbol emerged under her feet.

The pure-white sand swelled and seemed to explode, with a black, metallic leopard emerging from within. They were autonomous *shikigami* that had activated when they sensed Natsuki's approach. They attacked Natsuki from her blind side, independent of Kiriha's will.

With Natsuki unable to teleport, there was simply no way she could evade the attack. The black leopard's steel fangs glimmered as they attempted to rend the small-statured witch's flesh apart. However, it was Natsuki who spoke next.

"—Or so you feinted, using yourself as a decoy for your own trap. A fighting style suited for experts in anti-demonic beast combat, but alas."

The following instant, it was Kiriha who was slammed onto the sandy beach.

"Guh-ah!" Kiriha coughed, the wind blown out of her, which her ears heard only belatedly.

Natsuki, of course, was without a scratch; Kiriha's trap hadn't been destroyed—the *shikigami* hadn't reacted to Natsuki at all. Kiriha's *shikigami* had responded to the golden knight construct appearing behind Natsuki. Natsuki's Guardian crushed Kiriha's *shikigami* in its grip, blowing Kiriha away with hand pressure alone.

"I praise you for forcing me to use my Rheingold, Priestess of the Six Blades."

Natsuki spoke plainly as she examined Kiriha, covered in sand below. She spoke with the disinterested tone of a teacher praising a student barely avoiding a failing grade.

"Having made me go this far, I will not forgive a disgraceful defeat, Yukina Himeragi!!"

Kiriha's face contorted in humiliation as she looked behind her where Yukina ought to have been. Then, when she caught sight of the girl, Kiriha was at a loss for words. The Sword Shaman of the Lion King Agency was simply standing there in a daze, dangling her silver spear from her right hand.

During the time Kiriha had earned by risking her life, Yukina had neither engaged in a scheme nor laid a trap; she had simply stood there, absentminded and defenseless.

To Natsuki and Kiriha, the wholly emotionless look of her eyes resembled the water of a windswept lake.

She had beautiful skin and glossy lips. Her face, fair far beyond the norm, somehow seemed fantastical, beyond the realm of humanity.

"Tch…"

When Natsuki noticed the change in Yukina, her face registered nervousness for the first time. Setting eyes upon Yukina, standing there wide open, she launched a barrage of silver chains that bore down like the rain. Simultaneously, countless chains attacked from every fathomable direction—the sheer volume well beyond what human reaction speed could cope with.

However, without a word, Yukina evaded them all. She slipped past most of the chains with a minimum of motion, lashing out with her silver spear to knock away the rest.

It was the work of a god.

"Divine possession...in this situation...?!"

Kiriha had goose bumps over her entire body when she realized why Yukina had undergone the abrupt change. To counter the Witch of the Void's overwhelming combat capabilities, Yukina had opted to call down a god. She had made a powerful divine spirit possess her, and in so doing, she'd obtained power beyond human limit.

A Sword Shaman was at once a swordswoman and also a priestess with superior spiritual power. Even so, this did not mean divine possession was an easy power to employ. A single minor slip in control would cause the destruction of the Sword Shaman's personality; she would never regain sanity again. Or perhaps the divine spirit's power would run amok, likely inflicting a grievous calamity on the surrounding area.

Kiriha did not think Natsuki Minamiya was an opponent who needed to be defeated by running such risks—all the more because they only opposed Natsuki for the Fourth Primogenitor's sake. However, without hesitation, Yukina had resolved to call down a god. Kiriha's tongue curled at the girl's determination.

"What is this...?"

Natsuki, standing still before Yukina, scrutinized her with shocked eyes.

Her teleportation magic would not activate. Her materialized familiars had also vanished from sight.

All around Natsuki, white crystals danced like flower petals. Even while Natsuki watched, their numbers increased, filling her field of vision.

"Snow...? No... Divine Oscillation Effect crystals...?!" Natsuki exclaimed when she understood the situation.

The silver spear Yukina gripped in her hand radiated a dazzling glow.

With the vast spiritual power from divine possession coursing through it, Snowdrift Wolf had crystalized a Divine Oscillation Wave. The pure-white crystals nullified Natsuki's magical energy, preventing her magic from activating.

And the fact that Yukina wielded Snowdrift Wolf like so meant that she was employing the spiritual energy gained from possession of her own free will. She was in complete control of the divine spirit she had called into herself.

"This divine spirit... I see... So this is why you were selected as the Fourth Primogenitor's watcher..."

Natsuki boldly smiled as she narrowed her eyes at the dancing snowflakes.

Yukina gently swung her spear upward.

Her once-emotionless eyes had already returned to normal. Her face, which had been beautiful beyond human measure, had regained the cherubic look befitting her age.

Yukina shifted her gaze toward the golden knight construct standing resolutely behind Natsuki.

The crimson thorns stretching from the knight construct held the Fourth Primogenitor's wild and ferocious Beast Vassal firm.

When her eyes met those of the lightning lion, Yukina smiled slightly.

It's all right were the words formed by her lips. *It's all right. Victory is ours—*

"—Snowdrift Wolf!"

When Yukina swung her silver spear down, it became a giant blade of light that cleaved the air.

That light blew the golden knight construct away, rending the crimson thorns asunder.

Regaining its freedom, the lightning lion scattered pale thunderbolts and roared.

The pillar of lightning rose to the very heavens, erupting in an incredible electromagnetic wave. It was said that power utilities and machines broke down across the entire island, inflicting damage in the tens of billions of yen—

7

"Goodness… It seems I pushed that hardhead a little too far."

Natsuki, the adult version wearing a white shirt and a tight miniskirt, gently placed a hand on her forehead.

It was the stone cell inside the Prison Barrier. Outside the window stretched a crimson sky reminiscent of sunset.

From time to time, flashes of light glimmered in the sky, and the building shook from the echo of distant thunder.

Through his Beast Vassal's senses, Kojou already knew what had happened in the outside world. Regulus Aurum, freed by Yukina, had run amok, and its demonic energy affected even the Prison Barrier.

"Just like before with Yuuma, huh?"

Kojou smiled weakly as he spoke, feeling partially responsible for his Beast Vassal's rampage.

Yuuma Tokoyogi had once borrowed the power of Kojou's Beast Vassal to break the Prison Barrier.

Inside the Prison Barrier was Natsuki's dream world, and even the power of the Fourth Primogenitor could not break out. However, outside the Prison Barrier was another story. If you slammed it with enormous demonic energy, slapping Natsuki's sleeping body awake, the dream world vanished, and the Prison Barrier became corporeal again.

If Regulus Aurum continued rampaging in the world beyond, the same phenomenon would inevitably reoccur. For that matter, there was a greater than zero chance it would reduce all of Itogami Island to cinders.

The only way to prevent that was to send Kojou, the Beast Vassal's host and master, to put an end to the rampage. In other words, Natsuki had no choice but to set Kojou free.

"Well, fine. You pass." She smiled wryly.

Kojou quietly patted his chest in relief.

He'd achieved his objective of escaping the Prison Barrier, and it was fair to say he'd done it on his own power. Had Natsuki not accepted her defeat, he'd end up busting out by force.

"So you'll…let us go?"

"It would be troublesome if the barrier broke again, and Aya and the others were freed, so yes. Go wherever you wish."

With that timid reminder, Natsuki gazed at him, listlessly crossing her arms. Kojou unwittingly averted his eyes, for this made her eye-catching bust stand out even more.

Natsuki, gazing at Kojou's reaction with visible amusement, suddenly rose to her feet.

"But before you go...I suppose I will give you a special going-away present."

"N-Natsuki...?"

Kojou's voice went shrill when Natsuki's body drew unnaturally close.

Cleavage that did not rightfully exist poked out from the top of her white shirt. Natsuki gave her long hair an upward stroke, seemingly showing off her slender neck on purpose. From any angle, the situation looked like a female teacher seducing her pupil while giving a private lesson.

Thanks to Natsuki's body having grown so much, the fact that she still had the baby face just seemed wrong. Kojou gulped, swallowing as he gazed at her beautiful, doll-like visage.

He did have some idea why Natsuki was seducing him like this. "I will give you a special going-away present," she'd said.

She probably means drinking her blood, he thought.

If he crossed over to the mainland, there was no telling what dangers awaited him. It was better than not, if he could use even a single Beast Vassal once more. If he drank Natsuki's blood there, the chance was high that he could claim a Beast Vassal that had not yet acknowledged him as its host. However:

"W...wait a sec! You're an educator and stuff...!"

Kojou desperately tried to hold Natsuki at bay.

Even if she was all grown-up, Natsuki's real body looked like an eleven- or twelve-year-old girl's. He just couldn't bring himself to drink her blood. After all, the trigger for vampiric urges was lust.

He felt that if he gave in to Natsuki's seduction and drank her blood, he'd lose something precious to him as a person.

"What, this situation holds no appeal to you? In other words, you prefer my usual form to my buxom female-teacher form?"

"Er, the issue isn't whether I like this look or not...!"

"Well, fine, here you go."

That said, Natsuki pulled up a roll of photocopied sheets from the cleavage of her breasts.

Where did that come from? thought Kojou, thrown off as he accepted the papers.

"Um... What is this anyway?"

"I told you, didn't I? A going-away present. You intend to skip the rest of your winter break extra lessons, yes? So I prepared your homework in advance. You should thank me. It's due the next day of classes."

Natsuki giggled, explaining with her usual vainglorious look.

"Ah... So that's what it is..."

For reasons not clear even to him, Kojou sank into disappointment, hanging his head as if all his strength was spent.

Apparently, Natsuki had been teasing him from the beginning. Maybe losing the bet had gotten under her skin. Either way, it was the sort of thing she would do.

"What? Did you think I would let a sex-starved brat like you drink my blood?"

Natsuki looked down at the crestfallen Kojou with amusement, insulting him for good measure. Then, with her usual haughtiness, she arched her bust, smiling coolly as she said, "Well, I'll think about it if you actually graduate."

"Thanks a bunch."

Kojou half-heartedly parried Natsuki's words, unable to take her seriously by that point.

A moment later, his vision wavered—a sign of teleportation.

When he suddenly came to, the Natsuki in the white-shirted female-teacher look was gone, and the young-looking Natsuki stood before Kojou. Apparently, she was escorting Kojou out of the Prison Barrier.

"Do ensure you make it in time for classes after winter break."

Natsuki made the statement in a quiet voice, almost a whisper. The atypically gentle voice felt like a command to Kojou.

Make sure you come back.

"Natsuki..."

Without thinking, Kojou called out her name, speaking it like a word of thanks.

As he did, his face was assaulted by ferocious pain, almost like being punched.

"Do not address your teacher by her first name, fool."

Somehow, Natsuki's indignant voice sounded...distant.

Then Kojou awoke from her dream—

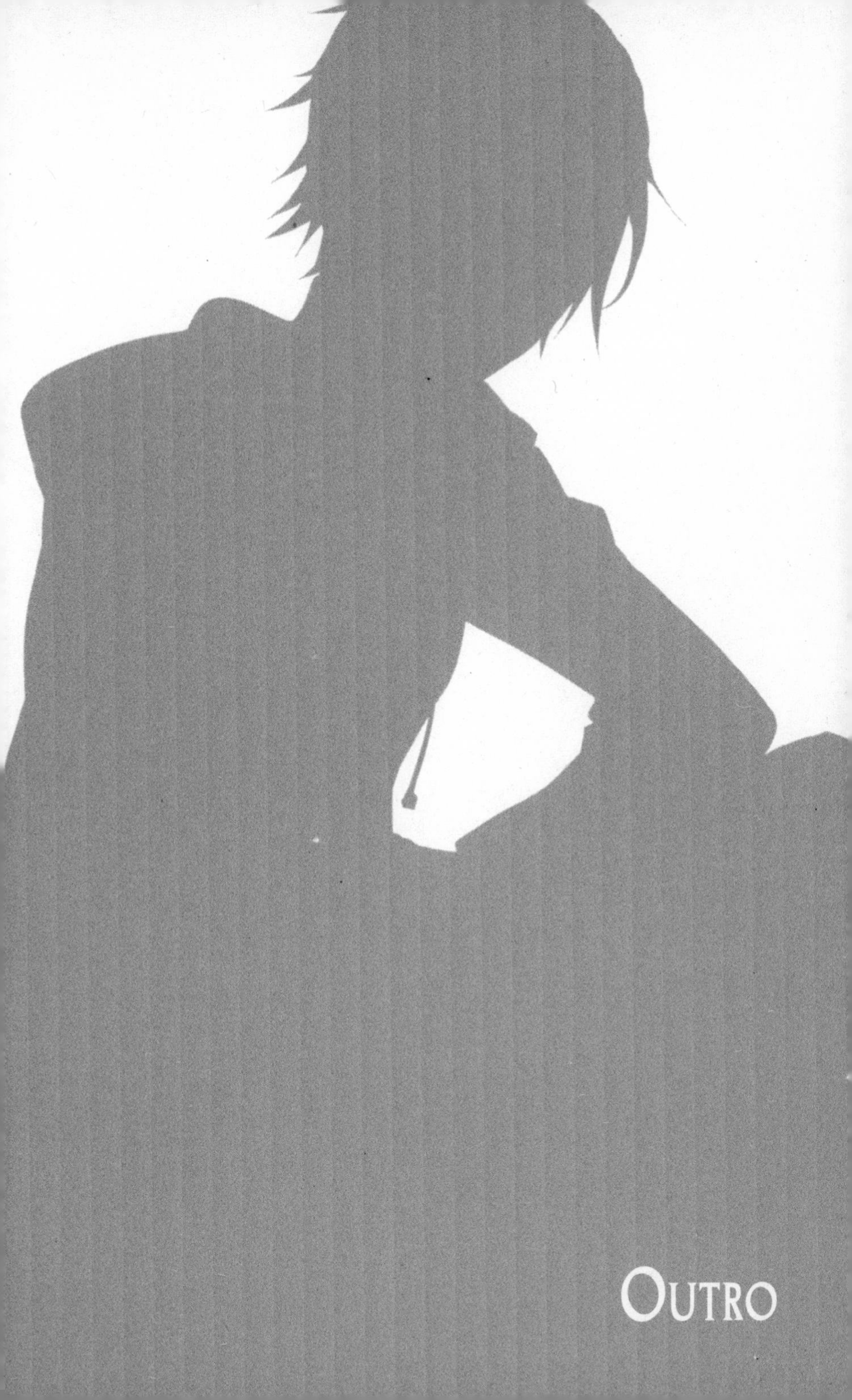

Outro

Kojou's back slammed hard against the white sand covering an artificial beach.

It had a water-break of bare metal and resin. It had a uniform, artificial skyline. The blue sky spread all the way to the water's horizon. These were the familiar sights of the man-made isle.

However, though he had returned from the Prison Barrier, he had no time to feel relief. A dazzling beam scorched his field of vision. The lightning lion, shrouded in a thunderbolt, was leaping right toward Kojou's face.

"Dowaaaaaaaaaa!"

Keenly fearing death from the incredible temperature, Kojou hastily dematerialized Regulus Aurum.

"I thought I was a goner..."

It was a Beast Vassal of the Fourth Primogenitor. Perhaps it was just playing with his returning master, but one graze of its claw would make Kojou's flesh boil away in an instant.

I wonder if I'd come back if my whole body evaporated? wondered Kojou, not particularly wanting to find out as he feebly sat up. He brushed sand off his entire body before putting his hands on his knees and rising to his feet. Yukina, just as covered in sand as he was, noticed Kojou and rushed right over.

"Senpai! You were able to escape the Prison Barrier?!"

"Well, kinda… You managed somehow—right, Himeragi?"

Kojou awkwardly scratched his head when he saw the look of relief on Yukina's face. Ensnared by the Prison Barrier, Kojou had been unable to do a thing to the very end. Ninety-nine percent of his getting out safe and sound was Yukina's doing. He could tell that much from seeing her all beat up.

"No. I believe Ms. Minamiya truly was holding back. I was unable to compete with her to the very end," she said, shaking her head in chagrin.

Kojou gently brushed some sand out of her hair as he said, "Pretty sure you did. Natsuki said we passed, y'see."

"…You remember what happened inside the Prison Barrier?"

People forgot many overnight dreams when they woke; similarly, it was extremely difficult to retain memories of what happened when leaving the Prison Barrier in Natsuki's dream world. Yukina knew that firsthand.

"Yeah. I'll tell you all about it later, Himeragi."

Kojou appeared distant while he spoke.

"Okay."

Of course you will, said Yukina's expression as she nodded firmly. When looking at Kojou, her face suddenly hardened. He felt like emotion was suddenly draining from her eyes.

At the same time, there was a prick deep in Kojou's nose, and he tasted metal. Warm liquid was dripping toward the corner of Kojou's mouth—a nosebleed.

"…Senpai, what did you do with Ms. Minamiya inside the Prison Barrier…?"

Yukina asked with a quiet voice stripped of all sense of warmth.

Kojou felt like it was hard to breathe as he hastily shook his head and insisted, "W-wait, you're wrong! This was just from Natsuki teasing!"

"Don't tell me you felt…vampiric urges…toward Ms. Minamiya…!"

Yukina, heavily thrown for a loop, seemed to be murmuring to herself. The odd strength in the fingers gripping her silver spear was frightening to behold.

"Y-you're wrong! Inside the dream, Natsuki turned into a grown-up teacher to match her age; her breasts were big— Ah, er, not that it really means anything, but…"

"A grown-up teacher…you say. Big breasts, you say. Is that so…?"

Yukina spoke in a very frigid tone as Kojou wiped most of the nosebleed away from his lips. To a third-party observer, it would not be clear whether they were arguing or flirting.

Then, at their feet, Kojou and Yukina heard what sounded like a deliberate throat clearing.

Kiriha, sitting on the sandy beach with her arms around her knees, looked up at the pair with a pouty look.

"I'm sorry to ruin the good mood, but aren't you forgetting something?"

"Ah, sorry. You were a big help this time around, too, Kisaki…"

Kojou, realizing that Kiriha was wounded just as much as Yukina, meekly bowed his head.

They still had to get Kiriha to escort them until they boarded the business jet. Earning her ire at that juncture would be bad.

Kiriha smiled maliciously, as if she knew she had Kojou over a barrel, and said, "Come to think of it, could you lend me a hand? My legs hurt, so I would be pleased if you could carry me."

"Well, fine. I can do that much…"

Kojou grudgingly nodded, picking Kiriha up as he was told.

Seeing Kojou carry Kiriha bridal style elicited a look of dissatisfaction over Yukina's face. Even so, she felt her own sense of obligation toward Kiriha, so she kept her words of complaint to herself.

As if to rub salt in Yukina's wounds, Kiriha put her hands around Kojou's neck and said, "You may touch me somewhat inappropriately along the way. It will be a bumpy ride, so such things are inevitable."

"It's hard to carry you if you're gonna say stuff like that!" he shot back in a shrill voice.

Kiriha drew her lips to Kojou's ear and said, "Incidentally, for reasons related to ritual sorcery, I am not wearing panties today…"

"Huh?!"

Unwittingly, Kojou stopped in his tracks, mouth hanging open.

Not wearing any. So she hadn't put on any to begin with. That's crazy. No, wait— If it's for a sorcerous reason, then she had no choice…? His mind concentrated, attempting to discern whether Kiriha's words were true from the sensations conveyed by his fingertips. Thanks to this, Kiriha's body warmth and physical softness weighed even more heavily on his mind. As a result, Kojou completely froze for two long seconds when Kiriha glanced back with a serious expression.

"I lied."

"That was a lie?!"

"Senpai…"

When Kojou, with a deeply wounded look, shouted, Yukina had sighed, staring at him in visible disappointment.

Kiriha giggled, at last seeming somewhat satisfied, but then—

"—?!"

—Kiriha's expression suddenly contorted out of fear.

Noticing the sharp change, Kojou asked, "…Kisaki?"

However, his words went unheard. The sound of the sea breeze, the calls of seagulls—he could not hear them, either. They were surrounded by complete silence.

It was all over in a second. Sound returned to the world as if someone had pressed a switch.

"What…was that just now…?!"

Kojou groaned in pain as he had the uncomfortable sense of being dragged to an unfamiliar place.

His mental process had been disconnected, almost like someone had torn a page out of a book. It was different than déjà vu or jamais vu. The discomfort was like watching a film that had missed a frame.

"Paper Noise…!"

Kiriha raised a shrill voice. Her entire body was trembling like a child who was afraid of the dark. Kojou could hear her teeth clattering.

"Hey, Kisaki?!" Kojou shouted in surprise as an unfamiliar figure wedged her way into his vision.

A lone woman was standing in the middle of the road leading from the beach to the next level higher. She wore a thin, veil-like silk, so he could not see her face, but it was clear that she was still young, probably little older than Kojou and the others.

She was wearing a luxurious priestess outfit adorned with countless gemstones. Even on New Year's Day, one could not walk outside in an outfit like that without turning heads.

And yet, until she had appeared close to them, neither Kojou nor the others had been able to detect her presence.

"Have we…met before? For that matter, where did you come fr—?"

Kojou asked, feeling like he knew this woman somehow. However, the woman in the priestess outfit did not reply.

She simply murmured in a gentle voice as if speaking to herself.

"The Witch of the Void is softer than expected. No…perhaps that is simply her nature."

"Why, you…?!"

Kojou's look became grave as he snarled. He didn't think she was some innocent bystander if she knew Natsuki Minamiya's alias.

"Senpai, please, get back…!"

Yukina drew her silver spear and raised her guard.

If the woman had used sorcerous means to suddenly appear, chances were high she'd used a teleportation spell or something along those lines. If so, chances were equally high that she was a formidable foe on par with Natsuki Minamiya.

Yukina glared, defensive against any kind of sorcerous sneak attack. However, the woman did not employ any spell. In a dignified voice, she merely levied a command Yukina's way.

"Stand aside, Yukina Himeragi—"

That instant, the Sword Shaman's entire body shuddered as if struck by an electric jolt. The tip of her spear, pointed toward the woman, swayed heavily from bewilderment and fear.

"That voice… You cannot be…!"

Yukina was petrified as the woman ignored her question, shifting her gaze.

Concealed behind the veil, the woman's lips loosened into a slender smile as she stated:

"It is a pleasure to meet you, Fourth Primogenitor. I am called Koyomi Shizuka, one of the current Three Saints of the Lion King Agency."

"…Three Saints…of the Lion King Agency?!"

Kojou's level of wariness rose by leaps and bounds when he grasped just who this dignified girl was. With Kojou on the verge of leaving Itogami Island, there was only one reason someone from the Lion King Agency, besides Yukina, would appear. She stood before Kojou as his enemy.

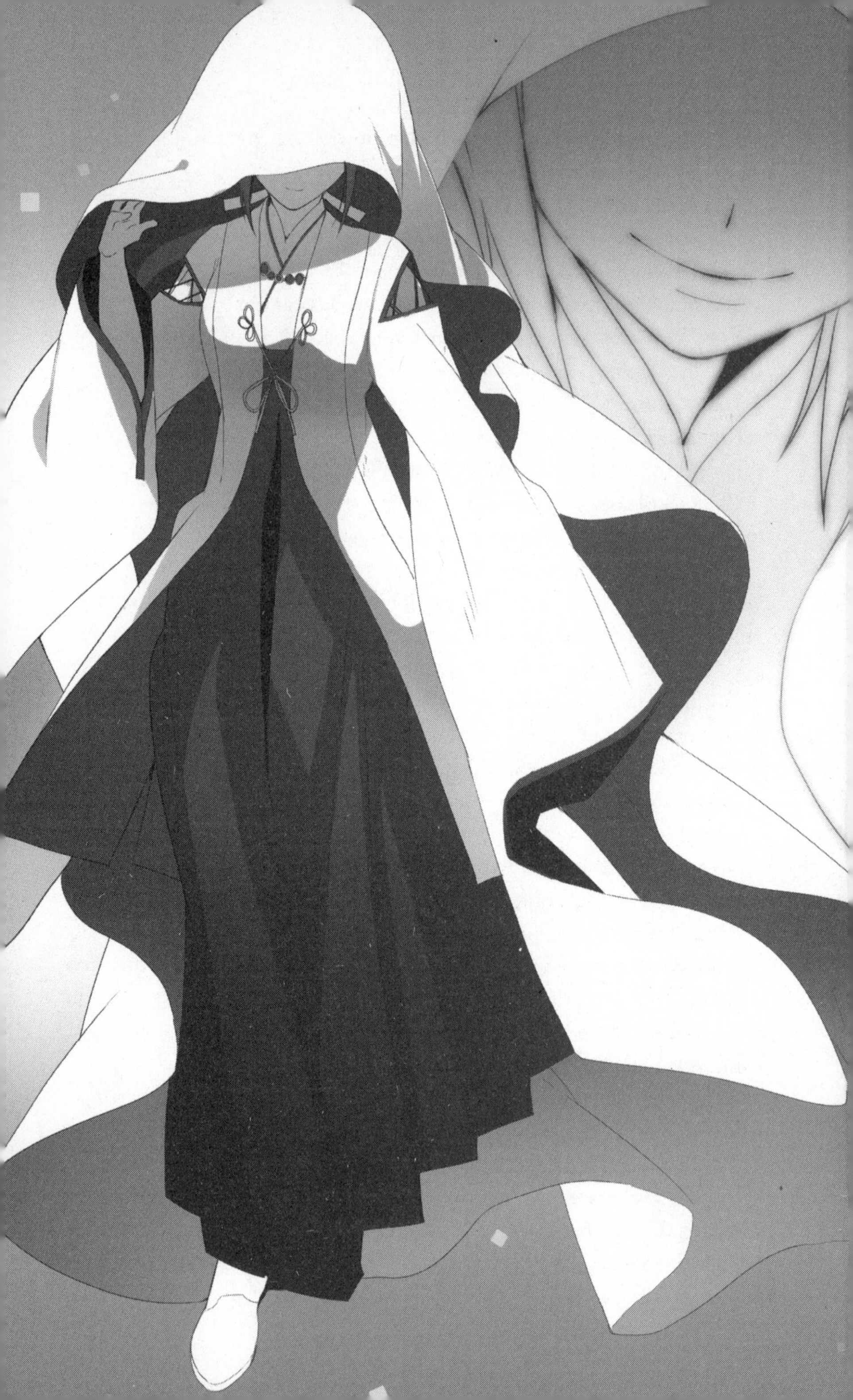

The woman in the priestess outfit stated calmly, "Unfortunately, by unanimous decision of the Lion King Agency, I have come to bind you to this soil."

"Senpai! She's dangerous—get away from—!"

"Flee, Kojou Akatsuki!"

Yukina and Kiriha shouted simultaneously.

For her part, Yukina thrust her silver spear into the ground, deploying a magic-nullifying defense ward around them. Kiriha leaped out of Kojou's arms and deployed her gray forked spear.

The next moment, the world was governed by silence once more.

Kiriha's body was sent flying as if struck by an invisible maul.

Pure-white sand scattered all about as Yukina collapsed to the ground.

Then Kojou was slammed into the concrete water-break hard enough to half bury him in it.

"Wha...?"

Kojou coughed, a large amount of thick blood pouring out of his throat.

Meanwhile, sound returned to the world.

Kojou didn't know what had happened. What he *did* know was that this was a completely different kind of attack than any normal spell. It wasn't like Natsuki's teleportation. The fact that the woman called Paper Noise had not walked a single step was proof enough.

It wasn't that time had stopped. It wasn't that she'd moved it frame by frame. It was more like...

...she was able to insert time that shouldn't exist, anytime and anywhere she wished—

Paper Noise.

"Please forgive me—"

At some point, Paper Noise had moved in front of Kojou. She held a silver spear in her right hand.

This was the secret weapon of the Lion King Agency that had rightfully been in Yukina's hands mere moments ago. In the hands of Paper Noise, Snowdrift Wolf—the primogenitor-slaying holy spear—glowed with a dazzling pure-white light.

Then, without any hesitance, without a sound, she swung that spear downward.

Gently, under afternoon rays of sun like those of midsummer, silence befell Itogami Island—

Afterword

Once again, there was a bit of a delay after the publication of the prior volume. It's been a while. Well, one way or another, *Strike the Blood*, Vol. 11 has finally made it to the shelves.

This volume has a fugitive theme to it, finally escaping the confines of Itogami Island. In a sense, Kojou has been protected by the Demon Sanctuary's safety net to date, but now that he must venture outside it, the circumstances around him will undergo heavy changes whether he likes it or not.

Those once considered allies suddenly turn into foes, or perhaps one ends up fighting side by side with former enemies. In hindsight, the peculiarities of the Demon Sanctuary were set in stone, so I was like *It'd be nice to show off a new* Strike the Blood *world*, and a meandering plan was formed.

To symbolize the various difficulties that Kojou and others must confront in the days to come, I first had to make someone unexpected stand before them as an enemy… That was the premise under which I used Natsuki, and really, it was fun to put her to work—she's so powerful that she hasn't had much screen time. I also wanted to portray Asagi's domestic environment, and I even managed to bring Kiriha back into the picture. From here, I'll be freshly portraying that which awaits

Kojou and crew on the mainland from the next volume onward. Expect great things.

By the time this book hits stores, I believe the last volume of the Blu-ray and DVD of the *Strike the Blood* anime will be on sale. Every volume comes with a novella I've written under the title of *Strike the Blood APPEND*.

The first to fourth volumes form one collection, *The Right Arm of the Saint (Cont.)—The Dollmaker's Legacy*, and the fifth to eighth form *Saikou Festival's Morning and Night*, a school festival story. When working on the *Strike the Blood* series, I've had unexpectedly few chances to write short stories, so personally speaking, I had a lot of fun writing them. One way or another, I wrote nearly enough for two stand-alone books, so I'd be happy if you picked them up when you have the chance.

Now that I'm taking a breather from all the anime-related work, I hope I can get my book publication pace fully back in order. I ask for your best regards moving forward.

Thanks as always to Manyako for handling illustrations and to TATE-sensei for handling the comic version in *Monthly Comic Dengeki Daioh*.

And let me express my gratitude to everyone related to the creation and distribution of this book from the bottom of my heart.

Of course, all of you who have read this book have my unreserved gratitude.

I hope to see you again in the next volume.

Gakuto Mikumo